ZERO DAY

AMERICA OFFLINE

WILLIAM H.WEBER

Books by William H. Weber

The Defiance Series
Defiance: The Defending Home Series
Defiance: A House Divided
Defiance: Judgment Day

The Last Stand Series
Last Stand: Surviving America's Collapse
Last Stand: Patriots
Last Stand: Warlords
Last Stand: Turning the Tide

The Long Road Series
Long Road to Survival (Book 1)
Long Road to Survival (Book 2)

The America Offline Series
America Offline: Zero Day
America Offline: System Failure
America Offline: Citadel

Dedication

As solitary a profession as writing is, no author does it
alone. A special thanks goes out to my editor RJ, to the
amazing beta team for all your valuable feedback and to
the readers who make all of this possible.

Book Description

The largest winter storm in a hundred years is barreling down on the northern United States. When it hits it will bring over a meter of snow and numbing arctic winds. Some are prepared. Most are not.

But something infinitely more dangerous is also on its way—a multi-pronged cyber-attack that will destroy the country's power grid at the worst possible moment.

Like millions of others, ex-cop Nate Bauer and his family are bracing for the coming winter storm, unaware that it will test them in ways they could never have imagined.

For hidden deep within the malignant code lies an even greater threat. One that will leave America shattered and in darkness for years to come.

When the lights go out for good, who will have what it takes to survive?

From the Author:

Before you begin this journey, there's something you should know. Consider it a warning of sorts. This isn't a story about Supermen or even Superwomen, the kind you've read about before, who consistently make head shots at a mile out and rack up body bags the way Imelda Marcos racked up high-heeled shoes. This is a story about regular folks placed in an unthinkable situation. The enormous stress they encounter as they are forced to navigate from one life-altering decision to another is something I pray none of us will ever have to experience. Some of the folks you're about to meet are truly prepared. Some think they're prepared. Some have no idea what's about to hit them. This is the story of what happens when each of them is put to the test.

Chapter 1

Nate Bauer came awake chilled to the bone. Next to him, his wife Amy slept soundly, her chest rising and falling in a slow, steady rhythm. There had once been a time she had insisted on cranking the heat to ungodly levels before bed. But somewhere around her fourth month of pregnancy, that particular pendulum had swung in the opposite direction. She didn't just like things cool now, she liked them downright cold.

But this wasn't cold. This was freezing.

Nate slipped out of bed and hurried across the icy bedroom floor to the thermostat on the far wall. She must have twisted the knob all the way to the left when he hadn't been looking. But when he got there he saw he had been wrong. The dial was at eighty degrees. The room should have been closer to a sauna than an ice box. His breath pluming out in white clouds, Nate headed for his cellphone, charging on the nightstand. As he passed the window, frosted over with frozen condensation, he skidded to a stop. A steep pile of snow had built up on the window ledge outside.

They had been warned about the coming storm. The forecasters had said the Midwest was about to get dumped on. There had even been a few inches of accumulation before heading to bed. Still, the sight before him now was something else. The snow that had fallen overnight had come in feet rather than inches, making it impossible to tell where the lawn ended and the road began. All of that was now a single, amorphous white blob.

Amy stirred and called him back to bed. Nate went, scooping up his phone with one hand as he pulled the blankets over him with the other.

"Everything all right?" she asked, squinting away the early morning light.

"The power's gone out," he replied, as calmly as he could.

She let out a long, tired sigh. "It's probably the snow."

Nate didn't answer right away. He was checking his phone and quickly noticed two things. The first was that his battery level was at sixty-eight percent. It had been closer to forty percent when he'd gone to bed, which meant it hadn't been charging long before the power had gone out. But the second thing worried him far more. There were five missed calls from his brother, Evan, an engineer at the local nuclear power plant. He normally gave Nate a heads-up whenever part of the grid went down, so hearing from him wasn't completely out of the ordinary, except his calls had started at two-fifteen in the morning and kept coming every forty-five minutes till now. That was strange. Very strange.

Nate flicked the screen with his thumb, pulling up his texts. There too, he saw his brother had been trying to get a hold of him. As if in slow motion, his gaze passed over a terrifying message all in caps.

POWER OUT. SUSPECTED CYBER-ATTACK.

Evan's message had erased all doubt. This was no ordinary power outage. The United States was under attack. But it was the sentence after that which sent long, skeletal fingers dancing up the back of Nate's neck. And he understood in that instant the situation wasn't only serious, their lives were in imminent danger.

Chapter 2

Day 1
12 Hours Earlier

The snowstorm that would go down as the worst in over a century began life as little more than a light dusting.

Nate watched as one of those white flakes seesawed through the night sky and settled on the gas pump before him. The coming blizzard was forecast to cover a huge swath of the country in several inches of snow and Nate wanted to make sure his pickup was filled to the brim before that happened.

The sign on the edge of Byron, Illinois, boasted a population of three thousand, but Nate knew the real number was far lower than that. The economic downturn in the previous decade had driven many folks to the nearby city of Rockford, and in a few rare cases, it had even driven some to take their chances in Chicago.

Most of those who'd stuck it out were employed at the Byron nuclear power plant, situated a few miles south of town. It was one of three plants in the area that not only powered the Windy City, but much of the state. And in another life, the power plant was also where Nate had worked. Head of cyber-security, that was his job title—at least for a while it had been, until he had pissed off the wrong people and found himself left scrambling to feed his family. As far as he saw it, corporate greed had been at the heart of the problem. But why drudge up the past when all it does is leave you seething over the injustice of it?

A sudden blast of cold wind slapped him back to the present. Nate reached for his wallet, removed his Amex card and slid it into the terminal. Right away, the display flashed an angry error message at him. He removed the card and reseated it, only to find the same thing. Staring around, he saw he wasn't alone. Others appeared to also be struggling. Like him, they too would soon be buried under a few feet of snow and were aiming to stock up.

"These things working or not?" he asked a man in a baseball cap standing next to a Subaru.

Subaru Guy shrugged. "Gotta pay inside, I guess."

Nate did just that, heading inside to find a line much longer than he had anticipated. Bundled in people's arms were candles, batteries, canned goods and in a few cases satchels of firewood.

This was the countryside, where folks were usually more prepared for the occasional act of God than their more urban counterparts. But even here, signs of complacency were showing themselves.

5

Nowadays, most everyone knew the average person's home contained roughly three days' worth of supplies. And that was assuming they hadn't put off a trip to the grocery store in order to binge on the latest Netflix series. In that regard, Nate was something of an anomaly. Perhaps it was his background in security or the fact that he was now somewhere in his mid-thirties or maybe that his wife, Amy, was now eight and a half months pregnant with their first child. Any way you sliced it, three days' worth of supplies was not nearly enough. Three weeks of food and water, on the other hand, made far more sense. Why not more? Well, as he saw it, only in the most dire circumstances would any emergency last longer than that. And if the worst happened, they could always stretch what they had left.

He'd tried convincing his younger brother, Evan, an engineer over at Byron Nuclear, to follow suit, but still hadn't managed to get much through that thick titanium skull of his. Hard to understand why, given his brother and his sister-in-law, Lauren, had twin boys to feed. Maybe if the coming storm was as bad as the weather lady said it would be, Evan might just come to see the error of his ways.

When the man before Nate finished, Nate stepped up to the cashier.

"Hi, Nate," the young woman said, smiling. She was young with fine electric-blue hair and pale sweaty skin.

"Evening, Candice. Busy night."

She glanced down at his empty hands resting on the counter. "No candles or firewood? You know the news says it's gonna be the biggest storm in a hundred years."

6

He nodded and grinned, dimples forming in his cheeks. "I heard. But I'm already stocked up, thanks. Just need some gas."

"Machines are down, I'm afraid," she told him, the corners of her mouth dipping slightly.

Nate pulled out his wallet and fished out his debit card.

"Sorry, Nate. Cash only tonight. Seems everything's on the fritz, doesn't it?"

He frowned. Cash was precisely the thing Nate was light on. He was starting to wonder if he was not nearly as prepared as he imagined he was. The lure of earning credit card points had slowly weaned him off of cash. Ninety-nine percent of the time that was just fine, maybe even smart. But clearly not so fine at the present moment. Nate plucked a lone five-dollar bill from his wallet and handed it over. "The old girl's thirsty, but I suppose this'll have to do for now." He glanced over his shoulder. "Maybe I'll try the Texaco on my way home."

Candice shook her head. "My friend Billy works there and he texted saying they got the same problem as us. Just saying."

Nate nodded, thanked her and left.

Five bucks would barely wet his truck's voracious beak. By nature, he had always been a pretty positive guy. Glass half-full type. The chances were good, of course, that none of this was a big deal. Once the storm passed and the bank machines came back online, he'd duck out and get the old girl squared away. There would always be tomorrow or the day after, he told himself reassuringly. It was a message steeped in a lifetime of wisdom and experience. Life in America was safe and reinforced by layers of security and redundancy. That was why major catastrophes were rare and when they did strike, they were quickly dealt with.

Nate filled up the truck as far as he could and headed home, plowing through a cold northern wind already swirling with snow.

Chapter 3

Nate pulled into the driveway of the bungalow he shared with his wife Amy and killed the engine. He was about to leave when his eyes flit to the rearview mirror. There he caught sight of a man he hardly recognized. The shaved head and goatee looked familiar enough, but not the crows' feet forming at the corners of his eyes nor the deep lines etched across his forehead. Nate had recently celebrated his thirty-sixth birthday and couldn't remember the last time he had taken a good long look at himself.

Maybe for good reason.

Like it or not, he was beginning to show early signs of wear and tear. At six-two and two hundred and ten pounds, most assumed Nate was some kind of narco cop—a suggestion that always made him laugh, but also one that wasn't entirely absurd. Way back, he had enrolled with the Chicago PD to become a cop and after going through the CPD Recruit Academy had soon been patrolling some of the city's most dangerous neighborhoods.

And yet the powerful urge in him to help make local communities safer had slowly been eroded in the face of all the suffering and needless violence he'd witnessed in those early days. Poor people murdering each other over the most trivial of offences. It was hard to process a nine-year-old shooting his friend over a comic book, not to mention the hardened criminals stalking the streets with near impunity. Once known widely as the Windy City, Chicago had recently earned a new name: Chi-raq, one that compared parts of the metropolis to a war-torn country. For reasons that were hard to fathom, the community he'd sworn to protect and serve was busy tearing itself apart.

It was around then he had realized big-city life with all of its dysfunction and rampant crime was not for him. So Nate had left law enforcement and, more importantly, he had left Chi-raq.

He and his new wife had resettled seventy miles west in Byron. It was here that he had spent time working as head of cyber-security for Byron Nuclear. Following a dispute, the company had let him go and Nate decided it was time to start his own all-purpose security firm. The company's original role had been in consulting, advising homeowners on how to set up surveillance around their properties. But this new career wasn't all about burglaries, since farmers made up the bulk of the folks around Byron. For them, surveillance was just as much about protecting livestock from wolves and other predators as it was keeping out burglars.

It hadn't been long before he'd begun getting calls from Rockford, a nearby city of a hundred and fifty thousand. The customers there weren't simply looking for alarm systems either. They were looking for an ex-cop willing to help investigate a delicate problem or two they were having. Nate certainly had the background. A black belt in judo and a brown belt in aikido meant he was just as handy with or without a gun. As it turned out, chasing down cheating spouses was a heck of a lot more lucrative than anything else he'd done to date.

Nate was out of the truck and halfway to his front door when he felt his knee begin to ache. He swallowed down the pain and hurried through the blowing snow, distinctly aware of his knee's predictive power over the coming storm. But that particular discomfort had nothing to do with growing older. It was a carryover from the terrible sports injury he'd suffered years ago in college, one that had killed his dream of joining the Olympic judo team. Although the crash itself had been over in a matter of moments, it had forever altered the path of his life. That was the true face of danger, wasn't it? Sneaking up when you were least prepared to face it.

Chapter 4

Amy was waiting for him at the door, her arms crossed over her swollen belly, a worried look plastered all over her face. At nearly six feet, she was definitely on the tall side. She'd been a captain on her college volleyball team. Blonde silky hair ran down just past her shoulders and whenever she turned her head it seemed to flutter like in one of those shampoo commercials.

Nate touched her belly and gave her a kiss, ignoring a fresh stab of pain in his knee. "How's my little girl doing?" He knew the reason for her concern. It blew in with him as he opened the door.

"She's been kicking up a storm," Amy said, no pun intended, laying her hand over his, watching as Nate shut the door behind him and stomped his feet on the mat. "Speaking of storms, I see it's already started."

Whipping snow was beginning to choke off any view of the outside world. The sight had an almost claustrophobic quality to it, given that sometime over the next twenty-four to forty-eight hours, they would be buried in their home. And when it was done, the only thing left would be to dig themselves out.

"Did you fill the truck?" she asked, a single eyebrow arched.

"I tried," Nate told her. "But neither the credit nor debit terminals were working. Five bucks was all I had on me. Once the snow's done beating the crap out of us, I'll go out again."

"That's strange," she said, biting her lower lip, a bad habit from her high school days. "I tried paying some bills online, but Bank of America's site was down. You don't think those two things could be related, do you?"

"A major bank and credit card on the same day?" he replied, nonplussed. "I seriously doubt it."

She let out a skittish burst of laughter. "Yeah, you're right. It was probably just a glitch."

He looked at her and smiled.

"You think I'm overreacting, don't you?"

Nate pulled her into a hug. "Not at all. I think you're one of the most level-headed people I know."

She laughed. "You need to get out more."

"Was there anything about the banks on the news?"

Amy dug her hands in her pockets and shook her head, sighing. "Only thing on the news is about the snowstorm. They say it's gonna be…"

"The biggest storm we've seen in a century," he said, finishing the sentence. "Candice at Casey's gas station already filled me in."

Amy's expression soured. "I'm sure she did. I see you two are on a first-name basis now."

13

"Now you *are* overreacting," he said, winking as he kissed her and headed through the front entrance and up a short flight of stairs into the rest of the house.

A bright red warning sign had been flashing in Nate's head since around the time he pulled out of Casey's and started for home, a carryover, perhaps, from his days on the force. That innate sense honed from patrolling dangerous neighborhoods. That same uneasy feeling soldiers serving in Iraq often described moments before an ambush—a street eerily quiet, devoid of people, absent even the incessant sound of barking dogs. Some soldiers said they could feel it in their bones, a kind of static charge filling the empty space around them.

Nate had been sensing the same thing, although he wasn't sure just yet what was causing the strange feeling. Could it be the snow? That seemed harmless enough. Life above a certain parallel in America came with an expectation of the white fluffy stuff in winter.

"Honey, where are you going?" Amy asked, moving up the stairs behind him.

"Got to check something," he replied, not wanting to alarm her. If he was wrong they could get on with their evening in peace. On the other hand, if he expressed his concerns and freaked her out over nothing, she'd be on edge all night. That kind of emotional stress was surely not good for the baby.

Nate made his way down a long, carpeted hallway to his office. The room was small and sparsely furnished. An L-shaped desk hugged the far wall. Above that was a bookcase with tomes on police procedures and books on the ins and outs of freelance private investigation work: *The Investigator's Licensing Handbook, Analyzing Crime Scene*

Evidence, Dealing with Stalkers and plenty more. Every patch of real estate on the walls was filled with diplomas and certificates. He had duplicates at his office in town. That was where he would meet with clients. Not here. This was his sanctuary.

This was also where he kept his guns, housed in a safe seated to the right of his desk. You couldn't follow people who were up to no good without expecting a little pushback from time to time. Sometimes a little more. But force was a last resort. Taking a life was no laughing matter. As any competent firearms instructor would tell you, if your finger touched the trigger, you'd better be ready to shoot. The acronym IAEF summed up his motto about as well as any could be expected to. It stood for "if all else fails". Wasn't it Clausewitz who'd once said, "War is the continuation of diplomacy by other means?"

Nate grew still until he heard the muffled drone from the other room as his wife returned to her television show. He'd meant it when he said she was the most level-headed person he knew. Calm, cool and collected, that was her baseline. He had tried not to show it, but seeing her on edge had rattled him. He returned his attention to the gun safe, running the combo and opening the door.

The contents included three weapons, along with several boxes of ammunition—his main sidearm, a Sig Sauer P320 with .45 ACP; his backup, a shortened version of the 1911, the Colt Defender; and his long gun, a Remington 870 shotgun loaded with double-aught buck.

Normally, the Sig with the Colt as backup was more than enough for the kind of work he did. That only changed if the subject in question was armed or a known felon. Otherwise the shotgun stayed home, since its primary purpose was for castle defense. The sheer intimidation factor that accompanied racking a round into the chamber was unmatched by any other weapon on the civilian market. Another reason it was such a hit: accuracy was far less of an issue than with other weapon systems. Once you leveled that barrel and squeezed the trigger, you were bound to get a piece of something.

The shotgun's reputation ran further than the intimidating noise it made. The mess it made of a man had helped crystallize the weapon's fearsome reputation in the popular consciousness, which in turn reduced the need to use it. "Talk softly and carry a big stick"—that was Teddy Roosevelt opining on foreign policy, but he might as well have been talking about a twelve-gauge loaded with double-aught buck.

The shrill sound of his wife's scream from the other room made the smooth skin on Nate's scalp draw tight.

Chapter 5

Nate came charging into the family room, his Sig in the low ready position, his practiced eyes scanning the room for threats.

His wife stood pointing at the TV.

He put the pistol away, his heart beating a racket in his chest. "Geez Louise, babe, you had me thinking someone had broken in." His eyes shifted to what she was seeing on the news.

"Police are calling it the largest ever cyber-attack on the US financial industry. Three of the nation's largest banks, along with a half-dozen credit card companies, were struck this evening by an internet-based attack of unknown origin. Although the banking industry has attempted to downplay the damage, sources inside suggest the funds from millions of bank and investment accounts may have been wiped out. At this stage, spokesmen from the financial institutions affected will neither confirm nor deny the claim."

Amy turned to him, shocked and confused. "What does that mean for us?"

"I'm not sure," Nate replied. The notion of a cold sweat didn't do justice to what he was feeling at this very moment. He felt his bum knee begin to buckle and set himself down on the couch.

Amy followed suit, sitting next to him. She took his hand and squeezed it. "How much of our money was sitting in bank accounts?" she asked, breathless.

Nate shook his head. "Between our personal accounts and the joint, maybe a few thousand. Just enough to pay the bills. Then there's both of our 401ks."

"How much cash do we have in the house?" she asked. Her mouth had gone dry, causing her words to stick together.

"Hard to say, but even if we had a million bucks hidden under our mattress it wouldn't matter."

"What do you mean?"

He squeezed her hand. "Whoever did this might have just wiped out the entire financial system. Most, if not all, of it is simply a bunch of zeros and ones held on hardened servers somewhere. If all that's gone, any money we have won't be worth the paper it's printed on."

"We don't know that yet," Amy said, hopeful.

All at once Nate heard a chorus of pings from his phone as texts started pouring in. Then Amy's phone started to ring. The landline soon followed. It seemed every communication device they owned had come to life at once. No doubt on the other end of the line was a mob of terrified friends, neighbors and family members, all reeling from the shocking news.

They didn't answer them, not right away. Nate set his phone to silent and set it on the coffee table before him. "There's something else too," he said. The TV was still on, the volume down as the talking heads circled like sharks in a feeding frenzy.

"What is it?" Amy asked and Nate could see from the look on her weary face she wasn't entirely sure she wanted to know.

"There was something about the way the news anchor explained what happened that struck me as odd. He didn't describe this as a robbery or a heist. He didn't say the funds had been drained from people's accounts and sent somewhere overseas to hackers in another country."

"But isn't that why hackers attack banks, to steal money? I mean why else…" Amy's voice trailed off with sudden understanding.

Nate was squeezing her hand, his grey eyes flashing with deep concern, and not only for their own future. They had just witnessed in real time the advent of an economic recession. Maybe a depression. Irrespective of that, the United States along with the rest of the world would feel the effects of this attack for years to come.

"This wasn't a money grab," he said, his voice tinged with icy anger. "Wasn't a bunch of greasy Eurotrash millennials or even a four-hundred-pound guy sitting on his bed. What happened was far too big, far too sophisticated, for that."

She stared at him and swallowed hard. "You mean like a state-sponsored attack?"

"Maybe even bigger. To pull off something like this, it would take more than one of our enemies acting in concert."

As former head of cyber-security at Byron Nuclear, cyber-attacks had been one of the many contingencies he'd planned for. Thankfully the plant itself was cut off and largely safe from any internet attack. Nate had quickly learned how the power company executives preferred electrified fences and guards with guns as a deterrent from the most likely attack, a physical one. They were so confident that when Nate had aggressively pushed them to wargame a cyber-breach, they had decided instead to send him packing.

But unlike the power plant, the banking system was infinitely more vulnerable. Even with their active measures in place, someone had still managed to get inside several key financial institutions. He had read a report back in his days at the plant that speculated foreign powers had already inserted malicious code into key industries and infrastructure throughout America. Likewise, our cyber-command had done the same to our enemies. It was the twenty-first-century version of mutually assured destruction. *You hit us, we'll hit you.* But it was one thing to trace the ballistic trajectory of an incoming missile back to its launch site and another entirely to trace the origin of a cyber-attack. The internet was a murky place. Uncovering the perpetrators and striking back would take weeks, maybe even months.

•••

The next few hours were spent watching cable news and speaking to friends and family. There was still no clear indication of the extent of the damage that had been done. The banks themselves were remaining surprisingly tight-lipped. But each new "expert" they trotted out only deepened Nate's already acute sense of urgency. The government had bailed them out once before. Nate wondered if they'd have to do it again. That was likely the best-case scenario.

After the first half hour, Nate had finally set his phone aside. His brother's wife Lauren was freaking out. It didn't help that Evan was currently working at the plant and might not know what was going on. There were too many unanswered questions, that was the problem. That was what made it so difficult to know the best way to react.

About a year ago, someone had managed to gain access to Amy's bank account and empty her checking accounts of the three thousand dollars she kept there. It was never made clear how it had happened. For days, she had wondered whether she'd clicked on an email or a link she shouldn't have. Amy was sharp when it came to technology. Wasn't her style to fall prey to the typical ruses—Nigerian princes desperate to offload their millions or fake lottery scams. Even the fake IRS calls so popular of late were given a quick and rather curt piece of her mind before she hung up. Through it all, the bank had remained silent. Ninety-nine percent of the time, when customers were the victims of fraud, they would launch a brief investigation and ultimately replace the funds. The question was: would the same thing happen now? Or was this particular hack simply too large and devastating to overcome?

Nate had been careful to spread his money around to a few of the major banks. That way if, God forbid, one of them happened to go down, he wouldn't be left completely penniless. Of course, he had never imagined

21

an attack sophisticated enough to bring down all the major institutions at once, not to mention the major credit card companies.

"How long do you think it'll take them to fix this?" Amy asked, chewing at her lip like she intended on boring a hole right through it.

"Soon, I hope," Nate replied. He glanced down at his silenced phone and saw six more texts had come in.

Amy drew in a deep breath. "I can't shake this terrible feeling that we've lost everything."

Nate leaned in and hugged her. "Not everything," he said and kissed her forehead. "I'm a hundred percent sure this'll all be resolved in a matter of days. There's simply too much on the line for too many people." A heavy weight pressed on his chest with just how easily the little white lie had come off. "Besides, we have more than enough stocked here at the house for the next few weeks or even more, if need be. I just hope our people are busy figuring out who did this and hitting them back ten times harder."

•••

Not long after, Nate brushed his teeth and got ready for bed. Normally the pistol would go back in the safe down the hall, but given the present uncertainty, he thought it best to keep it in the nightstand by his bed. He plugged his phone into the charger and scanned through the newest messages he had received. Most of them were nearly identical. Just about everyone he knew was losing their minds. Working in finance was a high-pressure job, anyone he'd known in the industry would be the first to admit it. No one had a sense of humor when it came to their own money. During the Great Depression, a number of folks who had lost everything ended up

22

stepping off the edge of a building. Steal a man's money, you might as well have taken his soul. It was a sad truism, but for many, there was hardly a graver wound one could inflict.

But there had also been other texts on Nate's phone. One or two had been about work. Clients asking about surveillance jobs and whether he'd found any proof of infidelity. Those were some of the lucky few who hadn't heard the big news yet. What they also didn't realize was that with no guarantee of being paid, Nate was putting everything on hold. Another reason was the weather. No one would be stupid enough to rendezvous with a lover during a blizzard. Especially not one like this.

Amy was still in the bathroom when Nate stood and went to the window. Much of the ground was already blanketed in several inches of snow. Down it came, fat flakes driven hard by the wind. He could hear it pushing against the house, making the windows creak and the joints moan. Not to mention his own human joints. There would be a major run on the banks tomorrow in Byron, Rockford and probably every other city in America. It didn't matter how much snow fell tonight. Plowed or not, the roads would be busy.

"It's really coming down," Amy said, coming up behind him, her belly pressing against the small of his back.

Nate nodded, but couldn't quite bring himself to say anything. The two of them were on the cusp of bringing a child into the world—their first. And a girl, no less. He should be ecstatic, and yet Nate couldn't help but wonder what sort of world would be here to greet her when she finally arrived.

Chapter 6

Day 2

The next morning, Nate lay in bed, staring down at the text message his brother Evan had sent him less than an hour ago.

POWER OUT. SUSPECTED CYBER-ATTACK. EMERGENCY SHUTDOWN PROCEDURES NOT WORKING.

He propped himself up on one elbow, rereading the message over and over, his chest growing tighter with each reading, his pulse galloping faster until he could feel the blood thumping in his neck.

Thump… Thump… Thump…

During a major power outage at a nuclear plant it was imperative to insert the rods and prevent the core from overheating. Failure to do so could lead to a meltdown. Anyone who had seen what had happened to the Fukushima plant in Japan or Chernobyl in Ukraine knew precisely what that meant. But the plant had backup generators to supply power intended to keep the core cooled, powered by a bank of batteries designed to last for several days and in some cases weeks. The attack had somehow managed to subvert all of that and perhaps more.

Nate fumbled with his phone, his fingers cold and stiff. *What's going on?* He typed the words and hit send. The progress bar stopped at ninety percent. Nate's cell and wifi signal were both full, so why was this not going through? He was about to call when the text finally completed. Nate knew cell towers utilized battery backup systems designed to maintain communications in the case of power failure. Although he wasn't sure how much longer they would last, especially once the rest of those affected woke up and found themselves in a deep freeze.

It was for that very reason that Nate had insisted they install a landline at the house. Even in the face of a major power outage, landlines can continue to operate for at least a week.

Nate sprang out of bed, threw on a pair of sweatpants and a sweater and headed for the kitchen. The phone was in a cradle on the wall. He plucked it up and dialed his brother's cell number. The line rang close to fifteen times, which in and of itself was strange since his brother's voicemail came on after five rings.

Reluctantly, Nate set the phone back on the cradle and leaned forward, his forehead pressed against the cold kitchen wall. What should he do? That was the question bouncing off the inside corners of his mind. They were now facing a fresher and infinitely more dangerous threat than they had last night, but with even less certainty on how to respond. First an attack on the banks and now on the lifeblood of the country itself, its power supply. Should they evacuate the area and head to some kind of shelter, assuming one even existed? Or should they wait to see if things became more serious? In his text, Evan hadn't told them to pack up and flee at once, which implied the quick reaction teams at the plant were actively working to get the situation under control. As a former head of cyber-security there, Nate knew something of the protocol. All non-essential personnel would be evacuated while men like his brother struggled to prevent a full meltdown.

Nate went to a large bay window that peered out onto the street, watching with dread as the snow continued piling up. The cold hand closing around his heart was making it hard to breathe. His initial instinct, the one he'd prepared for all these years, was to hunker down and wait it out. They had enough food, water and ammunition to keep them going for a few weeks. Staying put was also generally smarter than hightailing it into the woods. For one, you would be exposed to immense danger during the journey. Second, there was no telling what you'd find once you got to your destination, assuming you even had one. Living in the woods sure sounded romantic, but even that took a hardiness most did not possess. Besides, it wasn't a sustainable solution.

But the real dealbreaker they were facing was the weather. Grabbing a go-bag and fleeing into the woods in the dead of summer might be challenging, but at least you could sleep out under the stars. In winter, all bets were off. And Nate had to admit, every single one of his evacuation scenarios had taken for granted it would occur some time in the summer. Could that be because the vast majority of the research he had done tended to address that very scenario? Sadly, fleeing your home in the dead of winter, let alone during one of the biggest snowstorms in decades, was not a scenario often covered by members of the prepping community. And perhaps for good reason. If our enemies attacked us during the coldest months of the year, tens of millions would never live to see the following spring.

That very thought helped to crystalize another disturbing realization. None of what he'd witnessed over the last twelve to fifteen hours was coincidental. The country was under the largest and potentially the most devastating attack in its history.

But this latest stage involving the Byron nuclear power plant was beyond evil. Against all odds, the culprits had somehow managed to insert malware into the plant's security network. Lacking details, Nate could only speculate, but this had been precisely the reason he'd fought so hard to wargame such a scenario. It didn't matter that our nuclear plants weren't connected to the internet. Neither was the Natanz uranium enrichment plant in Iran and nation states had still managed to infect their systems with a worm called Stuxnet and destroy about a thousand centrifuges.

The theory was that the malware had been inserted via a corrupt thumb drive. It was a point Nate had brought up more than once to the executives in charge. After the company's president had ordered him to drop it, Nate had taken his concerns to the board of directors. The following day he'd been terminated from the company.

But that wouldn't change the deficiencies in his plant's cyber-security protocol Nate had witnessed. Even after the successful Iranian attack, Nate had seen thumb drives with the company's logo being used to move information from laptops to desktops within the complex. How hard would it have been for a bad actor working a low-level admin position to slip a corrupted drive onto someone's desk? All it took was for some overworked and unsuspecting schlub to plug it in and the worm would do the rest.

Another potential access point he'd identified was the hardware itself. Programmable logic controllers or PLCs are digital computer components imbedded inside hardware that's designed to control industrial processes. In 2007, during the Aurora Generator Test, a group of hackers took control of a generator and sent instructions via its PLC, causing it to explode. That should have been a wake-up call to the world that industrial sabotage no longer required throwing monkey wrenches into the works. The wrench was obsolete and with powerful tools like Stuxnet, the works could be destroyed from almost anywhere.

The attack on Iran's uranium production back in 2007 had been a clear victory for the good guys. But with Stuxnet's release, a Pandora's box of sorts had been swung wide open. Soon the same malicious code that had worked to such devastating effect against the Iranians was being retooled by our enemies and used against us. In a strange twist of irony, we had armed them with the very weapons with which to destroy us.

Chapter 7

"We're in trouble, aren't we?" Amy asked. She was standing behind him, the comforter wrapped tightly around her. A white plume escaped her lips as she spoke.

Nate stared outside at the blowing snow, weighing his options. Slowly, he turned and laid out the situation as he understood it.

"I just knew something was going on," Amy said, her blonde ponytail swinging about her shoulders as she shook her head. "I could feel it in my bones."

"And in my knee," Nate replied, trying on a weak smile and finding it didn't quite fit.

"Who have you talked to?"

He shook his head. "No one yet. I tried Evan, who was doing an overnight shift at the plant. But I haven't heard back. Cell calls aren't going through. What about you?"

"I got a text from my dad," Amy told him. "Looks like the power's also out in Nebraska."

Nate's own folks had both passed five years ago, their lives claimed in a car crash in Arizona.

"For now, we have plenty of chopped wood and a stove we can use to cook food on," he said, swallowing a sudden lump in his throat and heading into the living room. Once there, Nate stoked the dying embers and threw a few logs on and closed the door. The fireplace itself was an insert, which was more heat-efficient than an open fireplace and also provided a ledge that could be used for preparing meals.

"If we end up leaving, we could head for my parents' place," Amy suggested.

Nate wasn't sure. "To be honest, we aren't there yet. We should get ready in case we need to bug out, but I want to hear from Evan first. If anyone can get things at the plant under control it's him."

"And what if he's stuck there and can't get through to us?"

Nate could see Amy's mind was also reeling with frightening possibilities.

"I mean, Nate, this is beyond the worst-case scenario."

"Not yet it isn't," he said, calmly, doing his very best to reassure her. The reminder that he was dealing with a pregnant wife carrying his unborn daughter was never far from his mind. He would never let anything happen to them, even if that meant laying down his own life.

"So what now then?" she asked, approaching the fire and holding out her hands in search of warmth.

"We need to grab Lauren and the twins. She's at home alone and there's no telling when Evan will be back. I can only imagine how freaked out they'll be once they figure out what's going on. You and I will swing by, fill up both trucks with as many supplies as we can and escort them back here."

"You want her to drive back here in her own truck in this weather? The cab in the Dodge has enough room for all five of us."

"Hey, I know Lauren," Nate said, frowning. "She and Hunter don't pack light. Besides, we'll need room for the rest of the food. With four extra mouths to feed, the supplies I put aside won't last long. If we go slow, we should be fine. The alternative is I leave my pregnant wife at home alone and I'm simply not prepared to do that."

Amy nodded, staring at the fire with a mix of fear and dread for what lay ahead.

•••

Shortly after, Nate was outside by the pickup, bundled against the elements and furiously shoveling snow from the driveway. The accumulation was somewhere past his knees with no end in sight. He paused for a moment to catch his breath and relieve the pinch building in his lower back. The sky was diffuse, as though they were under a dome of old, weather-beaten glass. A bright spot above the nearby tree line marked the rising sun. It was still early, no later than seven am, but he also knew it would be dark somewhere around four pm.

As soon as he'd cleared a rough path from the house to the truck, he went to the garage. A gas can he kept for the lawnmower was about a quarter full and he dumped

31

that into the pickup. Needless to say, the idea of cutting grass months from now felt incredibly remote.

While he was busy outside, Amy was in the house getting ready and, more importantly, reaching out to Lauren. The two women spoke frequently over the phone. Nate had learned from experience that if he told his high-strung sister-in-law to move her tush, it would only magnify any anxiety she was already feeling. He seemed to have that effect on people. Nate wasn't sure if it was the combination of his goatee and shaved head—a thought he pondered as he pulled the wool cap down over his frozen ears—or the timbre of his voice that could just as quickly lower to a growl in moments of danger. His wife thought of him as a teddy bear, but she also knew it didn't take much for that teddy to become a grizzly.

Amy appeared, dressed in a long winter jacket and boots with matching hat and gloves.

"Did you manage to get a hold of her?" he asked as they headed for the truck.

She nodded. "Cell phones still aren't working. But I got her on the landline, thank God. She'd just seen a text from Evan and was freaking out."

"I'm not surprised," Nate said.

"Well, you can't blame her."

That was true, he admitted to himself as they climbed into the truck. He started the engine, the dashboard lights flickering on as the beast roared to life. His eyes found the gas gauge at once, willing that little needle to move just a little bit higher. It sat somewhere around a fifth of a tank. Enough for the trip they were about to take. His brother's place wasn't more than a few minutes away by car. Unfortunately, without power, the pumps at the gas station had stopped working as well, which meant all that precious fuel was as good as useless.

Nate backed the truck up, rolling her hefty thirty-three-inch tires over the peaks of blowing snow layering the street like waves on the ocean. Nate grunted. "I sure hope they aren't packing for a trip to Cozumel."

"Be patient," she admonished him. "I know you wanna keep everyone safe. Lauren understands how serious the situation is." She reached out to rub the back of his neck when she spotted the pistol in the center console. "Is that really necessary?"

Nate grit his teeth as the truck fishtailed through the heavy snow. "I hope not."

Chapter 8

Nate and Amy drove through the blinding snow. The wipers flicked back and forth at full speed and even that wasn't enough to keep the windshield free from the incessant accumulation. If a grown man were to fall over out there, chances were good he'd be covered over in a matter of minutes.

Adding to the mayhem was the sorry state of the roads. They hadn't been plowed, which wasn't much of a surprise. Neither was the ghostly absence of vehicles. It was early enough that some folks were still in bed. The rest, the ones already up, could no doubt see that the power was out. But a simple glance through their windows would offer a perfectly reasonable explanation why that was so. Had the sequence of events played out differently, had Evan not texted him about the cyber-attack and the problems they were having at the plant, Nate too might have joined them in their blissful ignorance.

Part of him was sad, but a larger part of him was thankful. The panic that was surely on its way would likely manifest in two distinct ways. The first group would choose to shelter in place. Given the weather, it was a response that made sense, assuming, that was, one had the supplies to outlast whatever this was. The second would be to flee. Not because of the reactor. Oh, no, Nate had full confidence Evan and his men would soon get the core safely shut down. After rushing out for additional supplies and finding the shops closed, and after suppressing the urge to break in and simply take what they needed—the rules of civility enjoying a somewhat longer life out here in the country—they would speed home and probably end up in a snow-covered ditch where they would soon freeze to death. On the other hand, were the dice to fall in their favor, they would likely pack up and head to a remote family cabin or a distant relative's place. Either way they'd be charting a path for a place well beyond the range of their vehicle's finite gas tank. Once again, they would likely freeze to death.

It didn't matter how many ways Nate played out the scenario in his mind. Up in this part of the country, the lack of power was nothing but an accomplice. The weather, that was the real killer.

After braving the deteriorating conditions another mile or so, they arrived at his brother's place. Nate cut the engine and watched his own gas gauge with no small amount of concern. The needle appeared to be a little lower. Was that possible? Yes, she was a thirsty girl, but they hadn't gone all that far.

"Fighting the snow and all that wind'll do it," Amy said, seeming to read his thoughts. He'd never understood the eerie way she was able to peer into his mind. He might have called it hogwash if, over the years, she hadn't demonstrated her ability beyond any doubt.

Nate slid the Sig into the concealed-carry holster at his side. The Colt Defender was in the center console. That one he hadn't mentioned to her. They got out, locked the truck and headed up what they assumed were the steps and stopped before Lauren's front entrance. Amy rang the bell and struggled with the screen door, wedged shut by a snow drift.

The door swung open a moment later. A wide-eyed and clearly panicked Lauren helped them inside.

"Don't worry about your boots," she told them.

Nate and Amy stomped their feet, casting off sheets of snow onto the entryway rug, shrapnel from the fifteen-foot journey between the pickup and the front door.

But the nervous expression on Lauren's face wasn't the only sign his sister-in-law wasn't being herself. Suggesting she was a neat freak was like saying Jack the Ripper had a fondness for knives. It didn't begin to capture the totality of her obsession.

Lauren stood before them in a clear state of confusion, white-knuckling a plastic laundry basket filled with clothes. Her thin brown hair was tangled about her as though she'd just been through the washing machine spin cycle. She was still in her pajamas: a well-worn, baggy pair of grey sweatpants topped by a Mickey Mouse t-shirt. Lauren was fit for her age. Went to CrossFit classes every Tuesday and Thursday. Said it helped to declutter her mind. But you would never know that now, staring at the woman before them.

"Where are the boys?" Amy asked, her voice calm and diplomatic.

"Upstairs packing," Lauren replied, touching her forehead, before peeling off for the stairs.

"Ma, where's my Battle Arena shirt?" Hunter called out from upstairs.

"The blue one?" Lauren asked, one foot on the bottom riser as she rifled through the laundry basket with her free hand.

"No, the black one."

"I have no clue, honey. Wear your blue one."

Born five minutes before his brother Emmitt, Hunter had recently become something of an internet sensation. It had started after uploading a video of himself to YouTube, playing a popular videogame. It didn't seem to matter he was only nine years old at the time and obviously too young to post on the website. At least not to the one point two million fans who now followed him, hungry for new videos every day.

Over the past year, the kid's natural charisma and love for a game called Battle Arena—where groups of players fought one another to the death on a virtual island—had somehow managed to translate into a tidy little business, enough for the family to move out of their old bungalow and into a two-story job with a finished basement and a dedicated games room, what Hunter called his office. Nate wasn't sure how playing video games could make you money, but it was hard to argue with the results. It was also hard to argue Hunter's success hadn't done something to alter and maybe even warp the existing family dynamic. Forget that now, as a ten-year-old, he was pulling in close to Evan's yearly salary as a nuclear engineer. Interestingly, most of that warping was affecting Hunter's younger brother, Emmitt.

As if on cue, Emmitt appeared, lugging a heavy duffel bag down the stairs. On the bag was an image of a cartoon character wielding two silver pistols. He set it by the front door.

"That your bag?" Amy asked.

Emmitt shook his head. He was a redhead, like his brother, with pale, delicate skin and freckles. But where Hunter had a modern haircut, long on top and shaved on the sides, Emmitt's hair looked more like a red mop without the broom handle.

"It's Hunter's," he replied. "At least, the fuh-fuh-first of many."

Emmitt had recently developed a stutter. Curiously, it only came out when he tried to say numbers.

Nate felt a surge of frustration rise up his neck and into his cheeks. He had read somewhere that children tend to balance each other out. If one sibling was irresponsible, the other would become more dependable. If one was crass and rude, the other would be kind and polite.

If there were any fundamental differences between the two boys, Hunter's parents had only served to magnify them. The way they indulged the kid had effectively turned him into a diva. It was a trend Nate had seen more and more these days. Parents afraid of disciplining their children, some even trying to be best

38

friends with their kids. He might not be one to talk yet, given his daughter hadn't even been born, but already he knew that wasn't the way he would do things. When your kid's the one telling you what to do, something's wrong. In normal times, divas could be irritating. In the present circumstances, they could be downright dangerous.

"Hunter," Nate called out to his nephew, his voice low and tinged with just a hint of menace.

Upstairs, the sound of rustling stopped. A second later Hunter appeared at the top railing, the boy's eyes flashing a distinct look of fear.

"You get one bag," Nate said, holding a single digit in the air. "We also need room for food and supplies. When I return, I want all of you ready."

Hunter stared back, some of the blood draining from his normally ruddy face. "Okay."

"Return?" Amy asked, flashing a less than happy look. "Where are you going?"

Nate nodded. "To the plant, to see Evan. Find out what the hell's going on."

Amy folded her arms. "You sure that's such a good idea?"

Nate checked his cell phone and saw there were no new messages or missed calls. "At this stage, we don't have any other choice." He reached into his pocket and handed her the pistol.

She looked down at it, unsure.

"Consider it an insurance policy," he whispered, leaning in to give her a kiss. "Until I get back. Now, see if you can't get these guys moving. I wanna be back home before anyone in town catches wind the crud's hit the fan."

Amy flashed him that disapproving look again and it wasn't on account of bad language.

Chapter 9

A blast of freezing wind slapped Nate's cheeks the moment he stepped outside. His first act before leaving for the plant was to gather any unused fuel from his brother's garage. Fighting his way to the garage door, the snow piled up past his knees, only reinforced how challenging it was to get anywhere on foot in powder this deep. Nate gripped the handle, lifted the door and couldn't help but laugh. If there was one thing his brother loved, it was filling his garage with equipment he never used. Before him was a pristine John Deere E100 seated mower, not a hint of grass caked on the wheels or side chute. By any measure, Evan's front yard was fairly small and his backyard was half the size. Next to the mower was a Cub Cadet top-of-the-line snowblower. Beside that on a nearby shelf was a brand-new chainsaw, and below that a gas-powered weedwhacker that might have seen action no more than once. Seeing all of this thoroughly neglected gear, Nate marveled at his brother's wastefulness. But he was also thankful. Each of them was gas-powered and their sacrifice would be put to a greater good.

He grabbed the syphon and gas can from the truck bed and got to work. In all, he managed to scavenge three and a half gallons. The Dodge, it seemed, would live to fight another day.

With that out of the way, Nate hopped in the truck and headed for the plant. It was exactly five miles away, far enough to provide something of a buffer should anything ever go wrong.

The journey was slow going and Nate was relieved to still see that hardly anyone else was on the road.

As Nate drew closer, he noticed a change in the road. Tire tracks. Several of them, all heading off Highway 72. Which meant a convoy of some kind had passed this way heading for the plant.

On either side of him were open farmers' fields, covered in a deep, white blanket of snow. The wind had died down a touch, which enabled Nate to spot the massive twin cooling towers of the Byron nuclear power plant in the distance. Thick clouds of white steam vapor that normally escaped through the openings were now gone. While that suggested the plant didn't have power, it said nothing about the state of the core itself. As he approached the outer gate, two guards emerged from a small structure, their weapons unslung and at the ready.

Nate recognized them at once. The short, portly guy on the left was Sam Hastings. Somewhere in his late fifties, Sam had been working at the plant since it opened in '85. The other and far thinner of the two was a chain-smoking, foul-mouthed, but lovable guy named Joe Santili. Joe was a joker who was always quick to share a smile and a tale of his many exploits, several of which had occurred at various dive bars in Rockford. If cigarettes didn't catch up with him one day, Nate was sure beer and womanizing would.

Nate stopped the truck and started to get out.

"Stay in the truck, sir," Joe said, gripping his weapon and leveling the barrel.

Nate did as they instructed and stuck an empty hand out the open window. "Take it easy, boys, it's just me."

Joe swung around, stepping onto the mound of snow beside the road. "Geez, Nate. You nearly got your head blown off."

Nate stuck his head out now, confident they wouldn't put a hole between his eyes. "I got a disturbing text from Evan this morning, but I haven't been able to reach him since then. I'm trying to find out what the hell's going on."

"I'm sorry to say, but no one's allowed in, even you, Nate," Joe explained. "They got all hands on deck. Sam and I shoulda been done long ago, but they ain't sending no one home. If anything, we got folks from the company showing up I ain't never seen before."

"What kinda folks, security personnel?"

Joe shook his head. "Big trucks hauling a bunch of generators and what not. But they ain't the big ones like we use. These were small. Like the kind you find at the hardware store."

That wasn't good. Nate knew the larger generators Joe had mentioned were not only industrial-sized, but incredibly hard to come by. If one broke, it would take months, maybe even a year to source a replacement. Looking past the gate, Nate saw teams of people in heavy parkas moving bundles of electrical wire. Others were running back and forth. The scene was frantic and like nothing he'd ever witnessed in all of his time at the plant.

"They're trying to patch the smaller gens into the system?" Nate asked.

"Yeah," Joe replied, his breath coming out in a thick plume of white condensation. "That's the plan."

"Any word on whether they think they'll be successful?"

Joe grinned. "I sure hope so, I got a Tinder date tonight. Heck of an app. Ever heard of it?"

Nate laughed. "Once or twice."

"She's an older lady, but you know what they say, right?"

"Maybe, but I'd prefer to hear what the engineers have to say."

Joe winked. "Right, well, you know those types. Ain't nothing they can't do when they put their heads together. A handful of new faces arrived with the generators. Got something of a war room set up. People are worried and all, sure, but if I had to bet, I'd say they'll fix this." Joe must have caught the doubt in Nate's eyes because he then said: "If you're thinking of evacuating the family, I'd wait." He motioned to the storm. "You'd be crazy to go anywhere. Especially in this."

"Listen, can you give Evan a message for me?" Nate asked.

Joe nodded. "Sure thing, boss." Nate wasn't his boss, not anymore, but it seemed old habits were tough to break.

"Tell him to call me, either on my cell or on the landline, and not to give up until he gets through. Will you do that, Joe?"

"Sure thing, Nate." All three men shook hands.

Nate got back in the pickup and leaned out the window one last time before turning around. "Stay safe."

Chapter 10

Joe's words were still ringing in Nate's ears as he made his way back to the others.

You'd be crazy to go anywhere. Especially in this.

Although it was clear Joe's lifestyle left something to be desired, it was hard to argue against the man's logic. A part of Nate, the emotional, guns-blazing part, had wanted to scoop his wife and extended family up and whisk them away. To where though? The small farm Amy's parents ran in Nebraska was one possibility. It was no secret his wife hated the city. That hatred had helped to fuel their relocation to Byron once the nuptials were over and done with. A farmer Nate was not, but that didn't mean he couldn't learn. And depending on how things shook out over the next few weeks and months, he might not have a choice. Unfortunately, planning more than a few days out was pure folly, especially given the hand they'd just been dealt. The first order of business would be to get everything back home and stored away. Then, with the boys' help, Nate would work to secure the property. There was no telling who might take advantage of the suspension of law and order to run amok, even if that meant fighting the weather to do so.

Nate pulled into the driveway to find Amy and Emmitt filling the bed of their own pickup. Eco-friendly smart cars were fine, but glorified golf carts didn't cut it, not out here. If you didn't have a single pickup, it meant you probably had two of them.

Nate stopped the truck, swung out and folded back the bed cover. With her hat pulled down over her ears and her cheeks flushed from the cold, Amy waved and began heading over. Foot traffic from the house had created something of a path through the snow, easing her journey back to the truck.

"Any luck?" she asked upon arriving.

Nate shook his head. "Not really. Although the trip wasn't a complete waste." He told her what he had learned and the message he'd left for Evan.

"A safe nuclear reactor will be one less thing to worry about," she opined, letting out what looked to him to be a large sigh of relief.

"Well, we aren't out of the woods yet," Nate said, tempering her elation. "But I have full confidence in Evan and his people. If anyone can prevent a mushroom cloud from forming over Byron, it's them."

Emmitt was back, this time with a box of spaghetti noodles, the bulk kind from Costco.

"He's a hard worker," Amy said with a grin. She was brimming with pride. "Doesn't hurt that he's cute as a button either."

Nate laughed. "What about Prince Charming?"

Amy shook her head and lowered her voice. "He was trying to pack his Xbox and I had to set him straight. Can't say I managed to stop him in his tracks the way you did this morning, but I tried."

Shaking his head, Nate said: "Good to see he's got his priorities straight."

"As much as Hunter needs some tough love, it might do well to go a little easy on him. The kids don't really understand what's going on."

"They aren't the only ones," Nate shot back.

"Well, there you go. For all we know, this'll all get sorted shortly and we can return to our comfy lives of baseboard heating and binging on Netflix."

Nate kissed her. Amy's lips and even her nose were like icicles, but it was great all the same. After all these years of being together, the fire between them still hadn't dimmed a bit.

They both went in to help finish up. Lauren was coming down the stairs as they entered.

"Does Evan own a firearm?" Nate asked. He thought he knew the answer, but hazarded the question nevertheless.

"Guns? He hates them," Lauren shot back. "You of all people should know that."

She might not have meant it as an attack, but Nate couldn't help feeling the sting. Her not-so-veiled jab was about his missing younger sister, Marie. It was a terrible wound neither brother had ever fully dealt with.

Amy put a hand on Nate's arm to calm him. Her concern, however, was unnecessary.

"Look, Lauren, I don't want to leave anything behind that criminals could steal and someday use against us," he explained, his voice measured and smooth. Lauren had an unconscious habit of pushing people's buttons. He'd learned that a long time ago. He had also come to understand, once he had gotten to know her better, that her comments were not born out of malice. She simply had no filter. If a thought popped into her head, she was more likely to blurt it out than she was to hold back and keep it to herself.

By eleven am, they were back home and busy unpacking. A shelving unit Nate had built in an unfinished section of the basement would serve as storage for the non-perishable goods. One of the few benefits of losing power in the winter—at least this far north—was that the outside could double as a refrigerator. It was for precisely this reason that Nate had gone back to Evan's garage before leaving and fished out two large coolers. Setting food outside on its own would only invite wildlife still active during the winter months. A cooler could help, but was still not a great idea. As anyone in America with a garbage can could attest, raccoons were experts at popping off lids to get at any food inside. And contrary to popular belief, raccoons didn't hibernate throughout the entire winter. Rather, they tended to store up body fat in the warmer months and sleep for several weeks once winter arrived. A cooler in the garage would solve that problem just fine.

Lauren and Amy lugged two recyclable grocery bags filled with food into the kitchen. A moment later, Amy shouted back, "Water's not working."

No surprise there. The act of treating water to make it drinkable and then pushing it up any kind of elevation required power. Much like the nearby nuclear plant, the water treatment facility also used diesel generators, which had probably kicked into action the moment the power went out. But these were only temporary measures, a stopgap designed to do the job on a short-term basis until the utility company got things back up and running. It was hard not to be shocked by how much of our modern life relied on electricity. Rattle off a list of ten things you did in a day and the chances were great at least nine of those depended on power. But shock or surprise didn't really capture the extent to which their lives were about to change, regardless of how long this lasted. It was downright scary.

That wasn't to say the water would remain off indefinitely. It was possible the good folks at the treatment facility were waiting for more fuel for the diesel generators they used. Another possibility was that the town was keeping them off, to conserve fuel until they had a better idea how long this would last. Maybe then they would turn the generators back on for set periods of time. That way they could continue delivering water for as many days as possible. If you were stuck on a deserted island, you didn't empty your canteen until you found a fresh source of drinkable water. As far as Nate was concerned, the logic was the same here.

But, like the refrigeration issue—a potentially deadly problem in summer—the cold weather could be used to full advantage. Buckets of snow could be melted in pots over the stove and even brought to a boil for at least a minute to ensure it was safe to drink. Of course, the duration of the boil depended on your elevation, a fact not many folks were aware of. The higher you were—cities like Denver, for instance—the longer the water needed to be boiled, which was one of the reasons residents there were advised to boil unsafe water for at least three minutes.

Nate was still in the garage setting up a spot for the coolers when Emmitt appeared at the doorway with food from the kitchen freezer. He handed it over and stayed to watch as Nate stacked it neatly, taking care to keep similar food items together.

"Uh, Uncle Nate," Emmitt said, his voice quiet and hesitant.

"Yeah?" Nate replied, still sorting.

"Are we gonna die?"

Nate stopped and spun, shocked not only by the words, but by the fear in Emmitt's voice. "Well, if everyone does their part, I'm sure we'll be just fine." He paused for a moment before returning to his work. "Why do you ask? Was it something your mom said?"

"Nah, not her. Hunter said the power's never coming back on and that we're probably all gonna die."

Nate felt his teeth clench together. "Where is your brother?"

"In the living room, sitting on the couch."

"On the... This is no time to be relaxing. Go get him, would you?"

Emmitt ran off and Nate heard him yelling after his brother. Hunter appeared at the garage door a minute later, rubbing his arms against the cold.

"It's freezing out here," Hunter complained.

"Close the door behind you for a minute," Nate told him. "Don't let all the warmth out." He looked at Emmitt, who was standing behind his brother. "Will you give us a minute?"

The door closed, leaving the two of them together.

"Did you tell your brother that we're going to die?"

A guilty flush filled Hunter's cheeks. "Uh, I'm not sure. Maybe. I mean, when do you think the power's coming back on? I have a pretty big tournament scheduled for noon on Saturday and…"

"You're going to miss that tournament. I'm not sure exactly how to say this, but the power's out in this part of Illinois and parts of Nebraska. Right now that's all we know."

Hunter ran a hand through his hair and cocked his head. "Ugh, yeah, that sucks. Listen, do you have a generator or something? The battery on my iPad is running on fumes."

Nate's eyes became glassy.

"Your truck has a USB connection, doesn't it? Can I plug it in there?"

"I really don't get it. I see your brother helping load bags in the truck and empty the freezer and you seem more worried about videogame t-shirts, tournaments and charging your iPad."

Hunter's eyes fell.

Nate heard a ghostly echo of his wife's voice telling him to go easy. He let out a long sigh, before he spoke: "Here's what I would like you to do. Go ask your aunt Amy if there's anything she needs help with. I know the canned stuff needs to be brought into the basement and put on shelves. And when you're done with that, there's a long list of other things I need help with." He curled the fingers of his left hand around Hunter's thin arm and gave it a gentle squeeze. "What I'm trying to say is, the time for games is done. I need you to put your big-boy pants on. It's time to step up."

His nephew glanced up at him and nodded slowly. The kid opened the door and went back inside. Hunter wasn't a bad kid, not by any stretch. He'd just been allowed to get away with bloody murder for far too long. The Jesuit Ignatius Loyola used to say, "Give me the child for the first seven years and I will give you the man." Hunter was already ten, but Nate hoped it wasn't too late to salvage the good that still remained.

"Sorry to interrupt," a voice said by the open garage door.

Startled, Nate turned on his heels, the palm of his hand pressing against the cold grip of his pistol.

A wall of snow more than two feet high marked the demarcation line between the garage's interior and the outside world. The figure was dressed in a heavy winter jacket and fur-lined boots. It was Liz Corder, his next-door neighbor. "Hope I'm not bothering you."

Nate straightened and went over to her. She was a rather petite woman, somewhere in her early seventies. She used to be an elementary school teacher. Her husband Carl had recently sold his insurance business. Now both of them were retired and enjoying every minute of it. "Bothering me? No, not at all," Nate said. "Just keeping busy." He looked around, grinning with incredulity. "Crazy, isn't it?"

Liz nodded and let out a soft little laugh. She seemed unsure whether he had been referring to the snowstorm or the loss of power or both. "I'll tell you, it's really something else. Carl tried to get a hold of our son in Chicago and hasn't had much luck. I wonder if the blackout's gone state-wide?"

53

"Hard to say," Nate admitted, and it was true. He knew the Byron plant had been targeted by a cyber-attack, but what role the weather had to play and more importantly the extent of the damage was still impossible to say for sure.

"Yeah, well, I was really coming to see if you had an extra candle or two."

Nate nodded. "Yes, of course." He ducked inside the house and returned a moment later. "I'm gonna have to dig a few out. Can I bring them over?"

"That would be great." She smiled, her eyes beaming back at him.

"Is there anything else you need?"

"No, that's it."

She turned and was about to leave when Nate stopped her. "Liz, I remember a while back Carl mentioned he used to operate a ham radio. Any chance he still has it?"

"Oh, goodness, that old thing? I suppose he might. You know Carl, always jumping from one hobby to the next. I'm sure he's got it tucked away in the basement somewhere."

"Will you ask him for me?" Nate asked.

She told him she would and pulled the sides of her hood in as she headed back down the driveway. Watching his neighbor make her way through the shockingly deep snow, Nate couldn't shake the terrible feeling Liz and Carl were not going to live to see the spring. He shooed the dark thought away, convinced he'd allowed a touch of Hunter's pessimism to briefly infect him.

Chapter 11

Nate and the boys were in the basement setting up mouse traps on the food shelves when the landline began to ring. Nate leapt up to the main floor, taking the risers two at a time. The phone on the wall was already on its fourth ring when he finally answered.

"Evan, is that you?"

His brother sounded weary and short of breath. "Yeah, listen, I don't have long. I tried texting and calling you again, but right now cell phones are pretty much useless."

Nate concurred. "That's what happens when everyone tries to call at the same time." He remembered the same thing happening after 9/11. It had taken hours for the cell traffic to slacken. "How's the core?"

"Excelsior Energy brought in a bunch of backup generators to replace the ones we lost in the cyber-attack."

"I know," Nate said, speaking rapidly. "I swung by the plant earlier and…"

"Joe told me," Evan cut in. A muffled voice called out from somewhere in the distance. Evan put his hand over the receiver. "I'll be right there. There's no time to chat right now, Nate. But so far, the network of gennies have been working to keep the core cooled. As long as they're topped up with fuel, we should be good."

"You should know," Nate said, "your wife and kids are here with us. Once things are back under control, don't bother heading home. Lauren brought everything here you're going to need."

"Okay, listen, I got to go."

"One last thing," Nate said, trying to keep his voice steady. "Should we be getting ready to evacuate?"

Evan let out a long breath. "Byron isn't the only place hit. From what I hear, the government's struggling to respond, but most of the normal avenues to warn the people of Illinois have been disabled by the power outage."

He was speaking about the Emergency Alert System (EAS), a warning folks sometimes saw on their TVs and cell phones, most commonly used to notify of serious weather events or other national emergencies. At such times, a buzzing sound would be followed by safety instructions.

"Stay by the phone. If there's a problem, I'll call you."

"It might just be rumors," Nate told his brother. "But there's a chance the outage might stretch as far as Nebraska."

Evan was silent.

A frantic Lauren stood next to him, doing everything in her power not to rip the phone from Nate's ear.

"Your wife wants to have a word." He handed the phone over. Lauren took it with both hands while the two of them spoke.

Amy's eyes were welling with tears. She wasn't one to cry, which made it all the more unsettling. He held her in his arms. "Evan said everything's under control."

"Maybe, but after lunch, Lauren and I will prep go-bags for her and the kids."

"Smart," Nate conceded. "I'll think of an evacuation plan should we need one." That last part was more bluster than fact, since he already knew firsthand the inherent risks involved in driving unplowed roads.

"I'll make one for Evan too," she said, her voice more even now. "Just in case." She then opened the fridge and removed a package of hotdogs and buns.

Nate headed for the back deck to clear the snow around the barbecue. He had the propane tank connected along with a spare. If they played their cards right, the gas they had could last for at least a month, maybe more.

When he was done, he ducked his head back inside. "Babe, hand me two long candles from the dining room drawer."

She did so. "What's this for?" she asked.

"Call it my good deed of the day," he replied and kissed her.

•••

The storm seemed to grow in intensity as Nate fought his way down the driveway and along the street. In the distance, he could make out the low drone of personal generators a few of his neighbors were using to keep the lights on as long as possible.

He pressed on, one labored footfall at a time. There was no denying this was one hell of a workout. Years ago, he and Amy had trekked through the Great Sand Dunes National Park in Colorado. This was long before the pregnancy, during the tour they'd taken around the country. To put a finer point on it, it was exactly a year after the injury that had taken out his knee and any dreams of Olympic gold. The dunes hadn't been forgiving. Not on his throbbing knee, nor on his wounded ego.

But snow, when it got this deep, was a different beast altogether. He would take the searing-hot sand any day.

When Nate arrived at Carl's door, the old man was there waiting for him.

"Hard to believe somewhere else in the world it's warm and sunny." Carl laughed, phlegm rattling around his lungs like a nickel in a tin can.

Nate returned the gesture. "Can't deny I was thinking the same thing."

"Come in, if you have a minute to spare. The wife's making some coffee over the fireplace. I hope you don't mind the instant stuff. The espresso machine's down at the moment."

"Yeah, along with most of the state by the looks of things."

Nate stepped in, closed the door against the cold wind trying to get in and then removed his winter clothing. He set his jacket on a hook by the front door and removed the candles he'd brought. "I hope these will do for now. I've got a big stash lying around somewhere. Costco was having a sale last year. Once I get a minute, I'll dig them out and bring you some more."

"That's very kind of you," Liz said, handing him a warm mug. The house was toasty.

Nate took a sip, relishing the tingle it left as it went down. "Hmm, what's in this?"

"Oh, just some twelve-year-old whiskey I had lying around," Carl said, motioning to a seat by the fireplace. They had an insert just like Nate. In fact, Carl had been so impressed after seeing Nate's in action he'd gone and ordered one for himself. His neighbor had a wide, friendly face with eyes that sparkled whenever he laughed at an off-color or somewhat dirty joke. His hair was white and curly and concentrated mainly along the sides and back of his head. They were a sweet older couple who had been close friends with his folks, John and Lydia Bauer. After his parents had relocated to Arizona, Carl and Liz had taken over the role of surrogate parents, which made the fireside chat seem normal, maybe even welcomed.

"Seems like just yesterday John and Lydia were living up the street," Carl said. "Do you have any idea how hard your dad tried to get me to go golfing with him when he was alive?" Carl snickered, this time a low, throaty business. "I never saw the point of it. Nor did the good Lord bless me with the patience, but your old man, oh, he loved the… uh, endeavor." On principle, Carl refused to call golf a sport and was prone to argue the point with anyone who dared to say otherwise.

Nate didn't take the bait. "Golf in Arizona is a year-round affair, assuming, that is, you can stand the summer heat."

"I never much cared for heat," Carl said and Liz agreed.

"He breaks out in hives," she said, smiling.

Carl ran his fingers along the side of his neck. "I get puffy patches running from my earlobe to my collarbone. Heck of a sorry sight."

"Had to hit him with an EpiPen once," Liz said, as if to prove the point.

"No, sir. I much prefer the cold." Carl stared at Nate, his eyes narrowing. "You can always throw a sweater on if you get cold. But when you're skinned down to your trunks and sweating your tail off, well, there ain't much you can do."

"It's too bad my folks hadn't shared your enthusiasm. They must have reached their threshold. Just couldn't take it anymore."

Carl leaned back in his recliner. The fabric about the arm rests had the look of a ratty old pair of slippers. "It wasn't the cold they'd had enough of," he said.

"Oh, not that again," Liz shot back, with noticeable exasperation.

"It's true, Lizzie. You know as well as me the Bauers struggled to live in that house afterward, pretending as though everything was normal. The mystery surrounding Marie's disappearance haunted them to their graves. That's the truth."

Nate couldn't believe Carl was bringing up his sister. "It's haunted all of us," he said, a touch more forcefully than he had intended to.

"That may be so, but her disappearance happened not far from the house, and when your parents were home no less," Carl said, leaning forward, his elbows pressing into his thighs. "That's not something any mother or father can easily forget or forgive. You were gone to university, but Marie was only a fourteen-year-old girl."

"I remember," Nate said, the pain squeezing his voice down to a whisper. And in his mind, that was how she would forever remain.

"Innocent," Carl went on. "And confident. Not to mention curious. Yes, far too curious. My point is, I think the memories might have faded for a while, but somehow, after a time, they found a way to come back and far stronger than before. Made it difficult, maybe even downright impossible to live in that house another second. They died never knowing what happened to her, that's the hardest part of all."

"Oh, Carl, why?" Liz chastised her husband. "Why can't you let it go? It happened a long time ago?"

Fun-loving as he was, when Carl got it in his mind to do something, there was no stopping him, come hell or a hundred-foot tsunami. "Living a lie never did anyone any good. He's a man and soon enough he'll be a father as well. It's time he got the truth, warts and all. And just like your sister's ghost your parents said they felt walking through that house, you've got a ghost of your own. One that's been following you for a long time. It wasn't your fault, Nate, and I wish for everyone's sake you'd forgive yourself and let the dead be dead."

Marie wasn't dead. Not to Nate she wasn't. But he stayed quiet, sipping his coffee and staring at the fire. The thought of jumping to his feet and storming out had occurred to him. But he also knew Carl was right. In trying to protect him, his parents had only swept an uncomfortable subject under the rug. What had happened to Marie was a terrible accident and none of it was his fault. He repeated the line over and over in his head, wondering whether that dark, gnawing shame would ever go away.

They sat for a moment longer before Carl broke the silence. "I suppose on the plus side, it sure is nice to be free of all those electronics, don't you think?" he asked, setting down his cup and adding in a few fresh dollops from a silver metal flask. "The wife's always on the Facebook. Tries to tell me it's so she can keep track of the grandkids in L.A. I used to believe her too until I saw her posting all kinds of seems."

Liz burst out laughing while Nate sat there puzzled. "Seems?"

"Memes," Liz corrected him. "And stop fibbing to the young man." She turned to Nate. "I don't Facebook nearly as much. Not since Deputy Foster pulled me over for what he called 'posting and driving'. I taught the little bugger in third grade and would you believe he hit me with a five-hundred-dollar fine?"

Now it was Nate's turn to laugh. "Posting while driving. That's a first for me. You're lucky you got to keep your license. I'd say ol' Deputy Foster did you a favor."

"Ha!" Carl said, aiming a finger at her, his lips curled into a devilish grin. "I told you the same thing, nearly word for word, didn't I, love?"

She grimaced in her husband's direction. "Oh, shush, you old coot. Nate doesn't want to hear you boast."

Carl turned his attention back to Nate. "I heard you were asking about the shortwave radio."

Nate set his mug on the table next to him. "I figured since the phones are out, we might be able to radio out to someone who knows what's happening."

"Seems a bit premature, don't you think?" Carl said. "A storm this bad is likely to blow the grid out here and there. We shouldn't be surprised if a few counties go dark."

Nate realized it was time to come clean. He began filling them in on everything he knew.

"A cyber-attack?" Liz repeated, the words dangling from her slightly parted lips. The fear Nate saw growing behind her eyes was just as tangible.

"Evan says the company sent in a special team of engineers to help keep the core from melting down. He assured me the situation was well under control and that he'd warn me if anything changed."

"So let me get this straight," Carl said, leaning forward. "You're saying someone did all this through a computer?"

Nate nodded, the corners of his mouth sagging as if to say, *Hard to believe, but true nonetheless.*

"How's that even possible?"

"I know it's hard to fathom," Nate told them. "But consider this. Over a decade ago, the government ran a test called Aurora where hackers broke into a secured system and sent instructions to a diesel generator to self-destruct."

"Oh, goodness gracious," Carl exclaimed. "And here I was thinking Facebook was stealing my wife away. I never even realized it could also pose a physical threat."

"Here's what's more worrisome. The plant is cut off from the internet for that very reason," Nate went on.

"So the only way inside was to somehow smuggle infected thumb drives past the gates."

Liz was shaking her head in disbelief. "An inside job?"

"Hard to say for sure," Nate admitted. "If it had Excelsior Energy's logo, all you'd need is for someone at a coffee shop to slip it into your pocket or break into your house and put it in your briefcase. We may never know exactly how it happened, but I'm hoping someone on the shortwave might have some answers."

Carl swallowed. The warm smile that never seemed to leave him had faded. In its place was a new look, teetering somewhere between concern and full-blown panic. "Let's head down to the basement then and see what we can find out."

Chapter 12

Carl and Liz's basement was a garage sale junkie's dream come true. Stacked neatly along every wall was furniture from the 1960's and early 70's—oval coffee tables with angled legs, a walnut cabinet covered in cobwebs and dust. This stuff had been down here so long, it had come back into fashion.

By a far wall was a narrow desk with a single seat. A ham radio sat on the desk. Wires ran down the back to a car battery.

"Lucky for you I had a spare battery in the garage," Carl said, some of that old joviality coming back into his cheeks.

"Lucky for us," Nate corrected him.

Carl nodded without saying a word. Instead he flipped a switch and a series of lights came on, along with the sound of static.

Nate grabbed a 60's dining room chair with soft padding and settled down into it. For his part, Carl donned a headset that covered his ears and rolled the dial. Sitting next to him, Nate heard the hiss of static, followed by the occasional blip of silence.

"This is something of a lost art," Carl began telling him as he continued to spin the dial. "Nowadays, it's mostly old guys like me who are into this stuff. The boys and I in the radio club couldn't help but marvel whenever anyone in their twenties would wander in. Of course, nine times out of ten, they were lost, looking for the seedy bar next to where we used to meet." Carl was gliding over a scrap of unusual noise when he suddenly stopped. He rolled back, going over it slowly until a man's voice could be heard.

"Howdy, friend," Carl said. "This is call sign Kilo Niner Bravo Golf Golf…"

The voice continued.

"I think it's a recording," Nate said, leaning in to listen.

"… further instructions. This is the Emergency Alert System. Please be advised, an internet-based attack has cut electrical power to several rural and urban areas in the continental United States. Residents are being advised to shelter in place and await further instructions. This is the Emergency Alert…"

"That's not very helpful," Nate said. "A list of the affected states would have clarified things a bit more, don't you think?"

Carl stared at him blankly. "Unless the whole country has gone dark." He changed frequencies and called out: "This is Kilo Niner Bravo Golf Golf, handle Two Bear, if anyone is out there."

The radio hummed static. Carl repeated the message and waited.

"How long does it normally take?" Nate asked.

"Depends. This isn't a cell phone."

"No kidding. Have you considered that maybe no one's listening?"

Carl called out a third time when another voice came on.

"Kilo Niner Bravo Golf Golf, this is Whiskey Seven Bravo Echo Foxtrot, handle Sharpie. You're coming in at five over nine into Santa Maria, California."

"Thank you, Whiskey Seven Bravo Echo Foxtrot," Carl replied. "Sharpie, we're in Byron, Illinois, and wondering how things are going in your neck of the woods, over."

"Not very good, I'm afraid, Two Bear. Power seems to have gone out here at approximately twelve minutes past two am Pacific Time. All phone communication is also down, along with water. Besides a single police patrol, at this point, no real sign of government intervention. What about you? Over."

"Appreciate that, Sharpie," Carl replied. "Over here in the Midwest, we are presently in the midst of a monstrous winter storm. Unlike you, we have yet to see any government response whatsoever. No doubt road conditions are likely hampering their efforts to check on folks and keep them informed. I'll be honest with you, it's quite disheartening to hear the outage stretches all the way to the Pacific, over."

"Not only us, I'm afraid, Two Bear. My understanding is the power is out from the northern tip of Canada to the southern tip of Mexico. Although I

67

can't independently confirm that assessment, it seems to be the consensus among the radio operators I've spoken to. Over in my neck of the woods, I'm afraid to say things are even more serious. The local nuclear power plant had a malfunction during shutdown procedures and forced a massive evacuation from the area. I'm just a few miles past the danger radius, but I've heard a number of people have already died."

Nate shook his head, reeling from what the man on the other end had just said. He felt his hands shaking and his chest squeezed tight. Kids nowadays had an expression for what Nate was feeling. As the kids liked to say these days, he'd been sunned. Shaken to his very core by the revelation Sharpie had just laid out for them. Carl was no better off. He continued to ask questions of the man in California in spite of the dry mouth hampering his speech.

They finished up their conversation soon after, telling Sharpie to stay safe. Carl was about to shut the radio off when he heard a fresh voice calling out. Carl replied and the two men shared call signs.

"Pleasure to meet you, Two Bear, this is Renegade in Illinois."

Nate asked if he could take over.

Carl removed the earphones and handed them to Nate. "Be my guest."

"Hey, Renegade," Nate replied, surprised and even happy. "This is, uh… Overseer. We're also in Illinois— Byron, to be exact. What's your 10-20?" The old cop call signs were flooding back in. Although they weren't utilized in the ham radio code system, Renegade went with it.

"I prefer not to say, if that's all right, Overseer. I've got a well-provisioned setup where I am and don't intend on giving away my coordinates. There's no telling in times like these what some desperate nutjob might be willing to do."

Renegade's voice was deep, and sounded cured from years of smoking and booze. He also sounded like an older man, somewhere in his late fifties or early sixties.

"Overseer, you sound like a smart guy. I take it you've got a handle on our current situation?" he asked.

"As good as can be expected," Nate replied. He told Renegade about the nuclear power plant meltdown in California and that the one in Byron was currently facing the same possibility.

"I've got nuclear and biological air filtration systems, so I should be fine either way. If I had a single red cent for all those doubting Thomases who snickered behind my back… I reckon it's safe to say they aren't laughing now."

"Roger that," Nate agreed, smirking. "I reckon they aren't. Prep for war and hope for peace, right?"

"Right on, brother."

Nate was about to let Renegade go when the man said one last thing. "Should things get worse, and I have every reason to think they will, you need to realize we're less than fifty miles from a number of ticking time bombs." He was talking about the nuclear power plants in the immediate area.

To the south were the Dresden, Braidwood and LaSalle plants. To the west was the Quad City plant. And to the east were the Cook and Palisades nuclear plants. All formed something of a ring around the greater

69

Chicago area. That sinking feeling in his gut told Nate this was where Renegade was going.

"Won't matter whether or not the snow lets up," Renegade went on. "The inner cities are already a powder keg on the best of days. Won't be long before the refugees start fleeing the chaos of the city and heading for the country. Arm yourself, my brother. Once the God-fearing, law-abiding folks are dead and gone, the desperate and the depraved will be all that's left."

Chapter 13

The light was fading when Nate returned home, his progress slow not only because of the high winds and whipping snow. He couldn't shake Renegade's warning that it wouldn't be long before the cities emptied out, bringing with them more than starving and half-frozen refugees. Mixed in with the desperate masses would be another group, this one far less worried about breaking laws, much less commandments. Nate's only hope was that the Siberian conditions would act as something of a wall. An image came to him of the ice wall in *Game of Thrones*, holding back hordes of White Walkers. It wasn't a pretty thought. And maybe Nate was even a little ashamed the visual had come to him at all. But if anyone arrived planning to harm him or his family, there would be no hesitation. And above all, there would be no mercy.

Nate scoffed a cold hot dog before commissioning Hunter and Emmitt to help take some of the wood stacked by the front door and bring it inside. For the pieces on top, that meant knocking the snow off them. It also meant twenty percent of his stock would be kept dry.

While he felt the food and water could be managed, Nate wasn't as confident about his wood supplies. Depending on how long things lasted, he might need to chop down one or two of the small ash trees in his backyard. Trees lined most of the roads here as well, so finding them wouldn't be hard. But knocking them down and sawing them up, well, that was another story. Especially in weather like this.

The sun had already set by the time they sat for dinner. The flame from two candles made shadows dance across their faces, tired and fearful.

"I wish Dad was here," Emmitt moaned, stirring his food listlessly.

Lauren patted his back. "We all miss your dad," she assured him. "But he's busy at the plant, making sure we're safe."

"And trying to get the power back on," Hunter added, a tinge of hope in his voice. "Maybe then I'll be able to make the Deathmatch tournament."

"Don't count on it, bud," Nate told him. "If there's a problem, he'll call." He turned to his wife, who had already finished her meal. She was probably the fastest eater he knew. "At least you kept your appetite."

She smiled. "I'm eating for two, don't forget."

"How could I forget? Speaking of which, how are you feeling?" He didn't want to worry about a baby scheduled to appear in two weeks' time. At least not now with everything else on his mind. The look in Amy's eyes made it clear she was feeling the same way.

"I feel like I have someone else living inside of me."

He laughed and kissed her. "Good answer."

An hour later, Nate and Amy were getting ready for bed. He'd added some wood in the fire beforehand so that in the morning there would still be embers.

Amy, dressed in jogging pants, a hoody and slippers, slid into bed and lay on her side.

"Slippers in bed, really?" Nate couldn't help but laugh.

She giggled. "I hate it when my feet touch a cold floor."

"I thought you hated too much heat now." He was confused.

"From the neck up, I do. As far as I'm concerned, everything else is fair game. I thought you knew this already."

He leaned over and kissed the side of her head. "That's what I love about you. Every day I learn something new." He paused briefly. "The Colt I gave you earlier. Where did you put it? I don't want either of those boys stumbling onto it and…"

"It's okay," Amy said, trying to reassure him. She knew Nate's past had turned him into something of a stickler. "I have it in the drawer next to my bed. In the morning I'll return it to the safe."

He nodded, even though she had her back to him and couldn't see the gesture. "That's fine. I have mine here as well. This is pretty much how we'll need to do things from here on out."

Amy rolled over and eyed him as he rested on one elbow. "You don't think we're in that kind of danger, do you? Byron's one of the safest towns in the country."

"Under normal circumstances, I would agree with you," he conceded. "But this situation is far from normal and may be worse than we originally thought."

"What do you mean? You're scaring me."

Nate drew in a deep breath. The last thing he wanted to do was to freak her out, freak anyone out, for that matter. But his conversation with those two men over the shortwave earlier—Renegade in particular—had shattered any illusion of safety he'd been clinging to. It had also shattered any sense that this was a flash-in-the-pan sort of event. It was one thing when part of Illinois lost power and something else entirely when all of North America went dark. He told her what he'd learned over at Carl's.

"Oh, my God, why didn't you tell us sooner?" She was now sitting up in bed, any hint of sleepiness long gone.

"Because I knew all it would do is scare the crap out of everyone for no good reason. Besides, I was going to fill everyone in tomorrow. When we were fresh and rested."

Amy went quiet, biting her lower lip. "That means everyone we know is…"

"In the same boat as us, yes. It also means we may get visitors from the city as things become inhospitable there. They'll be a trickle at first, but as the weather gets warmer, who knows how many will come."

"If this lasts until spring," Amy said, a quiver in her voice, "who knows how many will even survive?"

Her question was rhetorical, but Nate had already run the numbers in his head. And the conclusion he came to was just as frightening every time. "Whoever hit us did so at the worst possible moment," he acknowledged, his voice low with anger and wrath. "Come spring, some might survive—the industrious, the prepared and those willing to do whatever it takes. The real question is, when and if the dust settles, what, if anything, will be left of our great nation?"

Chapter 14

Day 3

The sound of clomping had invaded Nate's dream. A group of lumberjacks were swinging at a giant oak with the wrong end of their axes, swearing and jabbering at one another in muffled tones.

Nate opened his eyes and sat up in bed only to realize although his dream had faded away, the lumberjacks hadn't. There were people outside. Nate woke Amy from a sound sleep.

"What's wrong?" she asked, rubbing her eyes.

Nate was already at the bedroom door when he fed the magazine into his pistol and pulled back the slide. He paused only long enough to instruct Amy to get hold of the gun in her bedside table and stay put.

She nodded and did as he said.

Moving down the hall, Nate noticed the voices had grown fainter. He moved into the living room and peered out the window. There he saw an SUV in the driveway, parked right behind Lauren's truck. Then a pair of engines started—first the SUV, followed by another vehicle. Nate rushed for the front door. By the time he got it open, the SUV was leaving the driveway followed by Lauren's pickup, the latter going in reverse. The thieves must have broken in and hotwired it.

The pickup was about thirty yards out when Nate removed the safety and opened fire. He was aiming for the vague outline of a figure in the driver's side window. Of that first volley, one went high, the second struck the back window, forming a small hole, and the third landed about the middle of the driver's side door. The pickup swerved and then gained speed. Nate ran out into the deep snow. He wasn't going to let someone come onto his property and take his stuff without a fight. The next four rounds went for the driver with limited success. Two shots hit the front windshield, spiderwebbing it. He aimed the remaining rounds at the tires, hoping he might pop one and disable the vehicle. Nate kept firing until the pistol ran empty, but the truck just sped off. He could have sworn he'd hit the driver, but outnumbered and probably outgunned, he knew it would have been foolish to give chase.

Amy came to the door. "Nate, your feet! You're gonna die of pneumonia, for heaven's sake."

His empty pistol was still trained on the now empty road when he glanced down and realized he wasn't wearing any shoes, nor a jacket. But the stabbing pain in his toes and along the soles of his feet paled in comparison to the searing anger he felt over being

77

robbed. He'd emptied an entire magazine without neutralizing the driver.

This was what happened when you didn't spend enough time at the firing range, he admonished himself. He spun and waded through the deep snow on his way back to the house. That was when he realized the thieves had taken more than Lauren's truck. They'd made off with a sizeable amount of his remaining woodpile.

He cursed loud enough for the whole neighborhood to hear him. Once inside, Amy closed the door. Lauren and the others were up and gathered around them. Not a surprise really, given he'd emptied a magazine at her fleeing truck.

"What's going on?" Lauren asked, pulling the edges of the knitted shawl she wore over her shoulders.

Nate moved swiftly past them without saying a word, the legs of his pajamas wet and leaving droplets of water in his wake. He headed straight for the office where he kept the gun safe. He was a firm, almost fanatical advocate of storing weapons safely. He'd seen what could happen when the awesome power of firearms wasn't respected. Which made it all the more surprising that he was about to break his own cardinal rule—never carry loaded weapons in the house. Even the pistol in his night table hadn't been loaded. The distinction was a small one, but a distinction nonetheless.

Now, after what had just happened, he saw that it wasn't desperation that pushed people to turn on one another. It was opportunity. The men who had come to his house to steal his things weren't starving, not a mere twenty-four hours after the power went out. And as Nate had noted yesterday, there were plenty of trees to go around for anyone willing to get an axe and start swinging. No, these men were thugs, parasites who made their living off of others' hard work. Why chop a tree and go through all that effort when you could roll up and steal the finished product? Nate had known, had even been warned, that such people existed and that they'd be coming, but somehow he'd convinced himself living out here in the country bought him an extra day or two.

What had also become clear from his encounter was that a pair of pistols just wasn't going to cut it. Neither would a single shotgun, not at range. For now, however, it was all they had. Nate fed double-aught buck shells into the Remington, ensuring the safety was engaged.

He heard shouting on his way back to the living room. Lauren had just discovered her truck was gone. But her voice wasn't the one Nate heard. It was Hunter's.

"My iPad!" Hunter wailed in despair a second time, before becoming noticeably silent, as though he had suddenly realized he ought to keep his mouth shut.

"Did they break into the house?" Emmitt asked.

Hunter slumped onto the couch and buried his head under a pillow.

Lauren and Amy were completely confused, but Nate thought he understood what had happened. "Hunter, you asked me yesterday if I would let you charge your iPad in my truck and I told you no."

Lauren's eyes flared with sudden understanding. "Was that why you asked for the keys? You said you were going to grab something you forgot. Hunter, I'm talking to you."

His face reappeared, filled now with guilt. "The battery was running low and I wanted to charge it. I know there's no internet, but all my songs are…"

It was all starting to make far too much sense. "So you went out to charge the device you're still addicted to, even though it's practically useless. And let me guess, you left the car unlocked since you figured you'd be heading back to grab it anyway."

Hunter nodded with slow, painful reluctance.

"You didn't leave the keys in the car, too, did you?" his mother asked. "'Cause I don't see them anywhere in my purse."

"I don't remember."

Lauren glared at her son. When a ten-year-old said they didn't remember, it was about as close to a confession as you were gonna get. She was on the cusp of laying into him when a knock came at the door.

With one hand on the pistol in his waistband, Nate approached the door and saw it was Carl, wide-eyed.

He let his neighbor in. Carl's pants were caked with snow from the thigh down to his boots. He removed the knitted cap he was wearing and slapped it against his leg. "I heard shooting and came as soon as I could." The old man was out of breath and brandishing a military-issue Colt .45, the same service weapon he'd used during two tours of Vietnam, in '66 and '67.

Nate invited him in. "We're about to start on some breakfast if you care to join us. Getting busy might help to settle everyone's nerves."

"Very kind of you," Carl said, putting the gun away and hanging up his jacket. "But I promised the missus I'd make her favorite this morning. Eggs Benedict. That

80

being said, how well the Hollandaise sauce turns out using the fireplace stove top may be a different story."

Nate let out a hearty laugh, appreciating the much-needed release of tension.

After greeting the others, Carl turned to Nate. "Is there anywhere we can talk?"

"Of course. Let's go to my office."

Amy and Lauren were already heading to the kitchen to start breakfast. Emmitt wasn't far behind. Hunter, however, sat on the couch, a pained expression on his face. He looked like a wounded puppy. If he was hoping to evoke any sympathy for what he'd done, it wasn't going to come from Nate. "There are three people heading to the kitchen to help make breakfast. Everyone needs to step up, now more than ever."

"Okay," Hunter said, pushing himself up off the couch, his slippered feet whispering along the wood floor as he went past them.

"Not easy being a kid nowadays," Carl commented once Hunter was out of earshot.

"Really?" Nate replied, a little shocked by the comment. "I'd say it was quite the opposite."

"From a comfort point of view, you have a point," his neighbor conceded. "But the pressure they're under nowadays, neither of us had anything comparable. My son David says his little boy is already working on his college application strategy. The kid's at least a year younger than Hunter. And didn't you say your nephew has a website with a million followers?"

"A YouTube channel, yeah."

Both men shook their head.

"I don't remember having a million of anything when I was his age." Carl released a wet gale of laughter. "But seriously, think of it, Nate. He's still a kid and he's got a business that makes nearly as much as his dad. There's something unnatural about that. He needs a firm hand, no doubt about that, but maybe also a little understanding."

A slow smile spread over Nate's weathered features. "Be careful now, you're starting to sound like my wife."

That laugh again, followed by a pat on Nate's shoulder. "Hate to tell you, Nate, but in the smarts and looks department, Amy's got you beat."

Nate nodded. "Can't argue there."

Nate scooped up the shotgun and the two men headed to the office. They passed the kitchen and living room when everyone else was busy preparing breakfast.

"If anyone sees anything unusual," Nate told them as he passed by, "anything at all, you holler out and let someone know."

Hunter and Emmitt stopped what they were doing and nodded.

Chapter 15

Nate closed the office door behind him and set the shotgun down inside the safe, but made sure to leave it ajar.

"The reason I wanted to meet again was that since your visit last night, I spent some time on the shortwave radio, reaching out for people in the area. Seems some parts of the local government are still attempting to hold things together. Managing the town's response to the dangers posed by the nuclear plant has been one of their top concerns."

"Excelsior Energy has a whole special team there now," Nate said, wondering where all of this was going. "I don't see how a bunch of local bureaucrats can help."

"They can by putting together a backup plan."

The two men's eyes met. "What backup plan?"

"More of an escape plan really," Carl told him. "In case the worst happens." Carl rubbed his red-tipped fingers together. "They've assembled a number of school buses at the Byron Middle School on Colfax."

Nate scratched his chin. "I don't see what good that'll do if no one knows about it."

"No doubt, the blackout's made that difficult," Carl acknowledged. "From what I heard, they plan to send vehicles through the streets checking on folks and giving them the instructions in person. Not sure how well that's going to work given the snow isn't letting up and the roads are barely passable as they are. Either way, you can imagine they've got their hands full just getting the water back up and the generators up and running."

"Where will the townsfolk be evacuated to?" Nate asked. A pencil sat on his desk and he started spinning it, a habit from childhood.

Carl looked at him, incredulous. "What does it matter? How about anywhere but here? If the core melts down…"

"If there's a shelter nearby, we can get there on our own…" he started to say before he considered they were now down to one truck, which was dangerously low on gas and only had room for two. "We had two trucks up until this morning," he lamented.

"I saw they took a bunch of the firewood you had sitting out front."

Nate nodded. "We got a chunk of it moved inside yesterday, but not nearly enough. I've read many of the same books you did on preparing for the worst. Heck, you were the one who got me onto setting up a few preps here and there. Renegade said it too, over the radio. Once things get too dicey in town, folks will start heading for the country, whether or not they should."

"It's human nature, Nate. They did the same thing when the Nazis pushed into France during World War Two. Clogged the roads out of Paris. Ended up slowing down the very troops sent to defend the city. It was a disaster all around, but that's what people do when the brown stuff hits the fan. They clog up the works, even if doing so damns everyone else to hell."

"I just thought I had more time."

"You mean before the lowlifes came out and started wreaking havoc?" Carl eyed him. "I see why you'd say that. This isn't Chicago. Compared to its crime-ridden neighbor, Byron might as well be in a different country. You might have been more prepared than the average citizen, but you didn't count on the full reality of the situation. It's fine to have loose rounds in your pocket, but they won't do you much good if someone's charging at you from a few feet away. You see what I mean?"

"First thing I gotta do is keep note of my essentials and make sure I do everything I can to protect them."

Carl nodded with enthusiasm. "That's right. Store what's left of your wood inside somewhere. Keep a weapon on you at all times. Make sure your family's always on the lookout for danger and sleep with one eye open."

Nate was taking mental notes.

"From now on, someone approaches the house, you greet them with the barrel of that shotgun. This is your castle. Assume they're friendly and you could end up dead. And make no mistake, if someone comes here intending to do your family harm, you're the first one they need out of the way. Once you're down for the count, they can have their fun."

"Don't underestimate Amy," Nate warned him, only half-joking. "She's more than a pretty face."

"Well, her pregnancy might complicate her lethality…" Carl began.

"No, I can attest, she's far more lethal now."

The two men shared a smile. "So these buses you mentioned," Nate continued, bringing the conversation back to the subject at hand. "Where will they go? Chicago?"

"Goodness, no. No one's that cruel or stupid. The plan will be to head to Rockford. It's about twelve miles away, just outside the plant's danger zone should the worst happen."

Nate considered this. "Rockford's twelve miles in a straight line. By road it represents a twenty-five-minute drive."

"Perhaps under normal conditions. Doesn't normally take me more than a minute to walk from my front door to yours. But just now it took me five full minutes and I was dead tired by the time I arrived. Also, none of the roads have been plowed or salted. If you're thinking of getting your family out by truck, you run the risk of getting stuck on the highway. And if you do, it's not like you can call AAA to come bail you out. Those days are over, my friend. There's also a more obvious issue. With Lauren's truck gone, you've only got your Dodge left and it's a two-seater."

Nate shook his head. "Would you believe we were supposed to go test-drive a used Bronco down at Billy's car lot two days from now? We could have fit all our stuff and five or six people, no sweat. I'd consider driving to his house now, except I can't access any of my cash and either way, I couldn't fill the tank even if the truck was sitting in my driveway."

Carl's eyes were warm and compassionate. They were eyes that said, *Emergencies always seem to strike at the worst possible time.* "Well, the wife has insisted if push comes to shove and we leave Byron, we won't be chancing it on the highway."

"You'll get on the bus with the others?" Nate sounded surprised.

"Under different, much warmer, conditions, I wouldn't be caught dead on that bus. But that wasn't the hand we've been dealt. It's very possible the country's major highways have already become unofficial graveyards for many a poor fool who chose to flee his home and spun out or ended up in a ditch. That's all it would take." Carl made a clicking sound with his tongue. "I have room for three in my car if need be."

Nate thanked him. He didn't see any other way of making it work. All he could do now was to harden the defenses around his house and pray Evan and his people would keep them from needing to evacuate.

Chapter 16

Following breakfast, Nate assembled the twins to help with moving the remaining wood inside. They stacked it by the fireplace and when that filled up, Nate set some old towels on the floor and kept the pile going. An hour and a half later they were done. Hunter might have messed up earlier, but at least he was making up for past mistakes with hard work.

Amy brought them all a mug of water, which they gulped down greedily. On the fireplace ledge was a pot where she'd melted snow, bringing what was left to a boil. She'd then filled the mugs and let them cool to room temperature.

Boiled water tasted different from regular tap water, but Nate and the twins were thankful. It always seemed like a strange thing to be sweating when the weather outside was this cold.

Next, Nate planned to reinforce the front door. He had a metal rod lying around in the garage somewhere, remnants from a home renovation he'd started last year. He would use it to fashion a door jammer. The concept was simple, but incredibly effective. One end was normally wedged under the door handle while the other end was secured in a bracket on the ground one to two feet from the lip. Once properly installed, a jammer could even give a SWAT team with a battering ram a run for their money. And although some determined bad guy might eventually succeed, he was sure to stir up such a racket, he would alert the entire house. All in all, it was a low-tech and highly effective solution.

Nate was in the garage fishing around for a bracket when Lauren appeared.

"Listen," she began in that universal tone that promised an unpleasant conversation to come. "What are the chances we can get our hands on a generator? I looked around and was surprised you didn't have one."

Nate shook his head. "Generators make noise. Noise has a bad habit of attracting attention. That's the last thing we need right now. Look what happened this morning."

"Hunter messed up. I'll be the first to admit it." Her thin lips formed into a weak smile. She was trying to lighten the mood by pleading guilty right off the bat, but it wasn't working. "Anyway, I just wanted to thank you for…" She paused, apparently not sure what to say.

Nate folded his gloved hands over the top of the metal rod and let it take his weight. "Lauren, I've never told you how to raise your kids, have I?"

She shook her head. "Never."

"And I shouldn't. Not simply because you're their parent and I'm not. But also for the most obvious reason. I don't have a child, at least not yet. So I've been careful not to overstep those bounds. What happened today was not all Hunter's fault. He didn't tell those guys to rob us. He asked me earlier if he could use my truck to recharge his tablet. I told him no, after which he probably went and asked you the same thing."

She nodded. "You know kids these days. They can't live without their electronic devices."

"Maybe," Nate replied, working to keep his heartbeat steady. "But now we have to live without an extra vehicle. And mine only fits two. So if push comes to shove, we're three seats short of being able to make it out of here. Yes, it might just be a truck. Maybe with Hunter's salary he could afford to buy you all a new one. But it's looking more and more like that old world is gone. That truck might have been your ticket out of here. And now it's gone too."

"You think we've spoiled him, don't you?"

Nate wasn't sure if it was a question or an accusation. "I think you've been trying to make up for Evan being at work all the time. I think for a while, it probably felt like the right play. Who knows, maybe ten years from now, we'll be having the same conversation, except you'll be telling me I've been spoiling my daughter. Hunter's got a lazy streak and it's best to nip that in the bud sooner than later. He also put us all in danger. We need to start thinking like a group instead of everyone for themselves."

Amy appeared at the door leading into the house. "I'm not interrupting anything, am I?"

Lauren spun around. "No, not at all. Nate and I were just discussing Hunter."

Amy's eyes fell, as though she had a good idea how that had gone. "I wanted to let you know I'll be with the boys for a little bit. We'll be sealing the windows upstairs with clear plastic." Doing so would help keep out the cold and minimize the heat needed to warm the house.

"Sealing the windows?" Lauren repeated, as though Amy had been speaking in a foreign language.

His wife giggled. "Maybe you should join us."

He caught Amy's eye and he winked a moment before both women disappeared inside.

She was something special. She could keep a cool head in a crisis and help rally the troops after the dust settled. Looking back, it was really rather unnerving to consider how chance had brought them together. For years, the loss of Nate's sister had left a gaping wound in his soul. He'd been in university at the time, studying computer science and a rising star on the judo team. When she was alive, his mother liked to remind him how stubborn he could be. And he supposed if by stubborn she meant determined and never willing to give up until the job was done, then yes, sometimes he could be as stubborn as hell.

Which made his fall from grace all the more remarkable. Less than two months after his sister's disappearance, Nate had finally reached his goal and become head of the judo team. It didn't only mean a certain level of prestige, it also opened the door to the Olympics and after that sponsorship and an abundance of other possibilities.

The match where everything changed hadn't been particularly noteworthy. Nate had been mopping the floor with one opponent after another. Throw your enemy off his feet and onto his keester—in a nutshell, that was the goal. Nate could sweep in either direction. His shaved head—yes, even by then—and menacing appearance only worked to his advantage. His final match was a large guy named Peter Alexander. He hated people with two first names. There was no real logic to the feeling, especially since given names are given and we don't usually have much say in the matter, if at all. Pete was a heavyweight, just like Nate, except he was close to three hundred pounds, little of it muscle. Flipping a guy that big was doable, but your technique had to be flawless or bad things tended to happen.

A young girl in the crowd. That was all it had taken. She was the spitting image of his sister. Maybe it was her ghost, come back to him the way Banquo had appeared to Macbeth. Nate had seen her right as he had grabbed Pete by the lapels of his gi and was making to fling the big man over his hip and onto the mat. It should have been one big Pete mess on the floor, like flinging the Kool-Aid guy and watching him shatter. Except Nate had been the one who shattered. His left knee to be precise, pinned under all three hundred pounds of Peter Alexander.

That day his dreams of Olympic gold had also ended. As soon as the three surgeries on his knee were done, Nate had packed up all his stuff into a VW camper van and left Illinois, never a hundred percent sure why. Perhaps it was because he had lost the two most important things in his life. Day to day, he found himself searching for a reason to get up in the morning, maybe even a reason to live. He'd discovered that reason three weeks later while working on a family farm in Nebraska.

Or rather, that reason had discovered him. Amy had been a lot younger then and far more naive. They both had been.

When his work on the farm was done, he'd convinced her to travel with him. He had gotten to know the family in the months he'd been working there and Amy's father knew him as an honorable man who would defend his daughter with his dying breath. The two of them had left to see the rest of the country. There was a big old world out there and to a couple of kids approaching their mid-twenties, it seemed an awful shame to let it go to waste.

Still physically in the garage, but wavering somewhere between past and present, Nate heard a voice call out from somewhere far away. He turned and saw his sister's face, smiling back at him. She looked happy, proud that he'd travelled through that dark night of the soul and come out the other side. Life was a series of tests. That was a lesson Nate had learned early on. Some passed, some failed, but everyone played the game, whether they wanted to or not. Nate could see that life was at it again. They were being tested and this time, it would be the biggest test of all.

Chapter 17

Nate was standing on the front porch, testing out the small white Geiger counter he'd bought at an online prepping depot two months ago. A cord led from the device to a five-inch wand. After inserting a fresh set of batteries, Nate turned the knob on the Geiger counter and held the wand out. The device made a few tiny crackling sounds. The dial twitched ever so slightly.

Footsteps thudded from inside the house a second before the door swung open. It was Amy and she was out of breath. "Evan's on the phone."

Nate slid the device into his jacket pocket and hurried to the phone. "Tell me you have good news." Nate said, trying to steady his own breathing.

"The situation seems to be under control," Evan told him. He sounded relieved, but incredibly weary. "Once the latest delivery of diesel for the generators arrives, that'll buy us another forty-eight hours. There's something you should know. This same struggle hasn't gone so well in other parts of the country. There have been meltdowns. One in California and…"

"I know," Nate cut in. "A neighbor of ours has a shortwave we've been using to collect information from the rest of the country. This isn't isolated to Illinois or even to the Midwest. The power's out in all of North America."

The line was silent.

"You knew, didn't you?" Nate said, accusingly.

"I can't say what I know," Evan replied, enigmatically. "The military arrived this morning in giant APCs. They brought their own engineers and have been making our lives a living hell, questioning every decision we've made. Wasting time instead of giving us medals for saving the county. If they just stick to the protocol I laid out, we should be fine."

Nate told him about the evacuation plan.

"Rockford, eh? Well, we're not quite there yet."

"Hey, if the military's so keen to take over, why don't you let them and come home?" There was a touch of sadness and desperation in Nate's voice.

"Don't worry, big brother. Someone's gotta watch the farm. You just make sure the house is nice and warm for when I make it out. I haven't seen a bar of soap in far too long." He might just as well have been describing a stint at a maximum-security prison.

Nate laughed. "Would you believe it's only been forty-eight hours since the lights went out?"

His brother returned the gesture with even more enthusiasm. "Forty-eight hours might as well be an eternity when you're living one second to the next."

And with that, Nate gave Evan his customary farewell. "Stay safe, bro."

Chapter 18

Nate was by the fireplace, nursing a steaming mug of instant coffee—one he couldn't remember ever tasting quite so good—when he felt the ground shake violently beneath his feet. That strange and unsettling feeling was followed a second later by a loud boom that rattled the windows and shook the house.

Amy called up from the basement in alarm. She had been grabbing a few items for dinner when the concussive blast wave from the explosion had struck them.

Hunter skidded in from the living room, flipping aside the chocolate-colored fleece blanket acting as a heat barrier as he blew past it.

"Oh, my God, did you feel that?" he shouted, eyes wide, standing in dramatic contrast to his freckled cheeks. "I think we're under attack. Those guys are back."

"Hunter, relax!" Nate barked, already by the window and scanning the empty snow drifts outside. The assailants hadn't returned. A detonation that strong could only mean one thing. Reactors number one and perhaps two at the Byron nuclear power plant had just exploded.

The nightmare scenario was happening. The proverbial bullet he had let himself believe they had dodged might have struck after all.

In a flash, Nate was dressed in his winter parka, poised on the back deck. Deep lines formed along his brow over what he was seeing in the distance.

First Amy, then Lauren, and finally the twins ran out to watch. Two generations of Bauers stood transfixed at the same nightmarish scene. Emmitt's head was tilted back, his jaw hanging open in bewilderment.

High above the tree line a billowing black cloud rose into the sky, its upper edges spreading ominously outward with every second that passed.

With fingers numbed by a combination of cold and terror, Nate fished the Geiger out of his pocket and switched it on. The Geiger came to life almost at once, spitting out a loud crackling sound.

"We need to leave and right away," Nate told them, heading back in. Hunter's thoughtless and dangerous negligence leaving the keys in the family car had just made their situation infinitely worse.

For its part, the explosion at the plant had distilled the present moment to a single point. All of the safety features they'd tried implementing these last forty-eight hours had failed in critical and disastrous fashion. It wasn't much of a logical leap to assume the core had melted down and was in the process of spreading a deadly aura of radiation over the entire area.

"Kids," Amy shouted. "Run to your rooms and grab your go-bags, just like I taught you."

Nearby, Lauren was trying to hold herself together. "We aren't coming back any time soon, so take whatever you can carry."

Nate had a list of his own which included the shotgun and a duffel bag filled with ammo. He then sprinted into the basement and the shelves filled with food, loading up with everything he could carry. Wherever they were headed, he wouldn't take for granted that food would be plentiful.

Faced with such a dire predicament, their choice was simple enough. Either they fled with their go-bags and headed for the evacuation bus he had discussed with Carl, or they could take their chances on their own. The pickup had two seats, with maybe a third seat up front for one of the twins. That meant Lauren and one of the other boys would be sitting in the flatbed, covered in blankets, hoping for the best. If anything went wrong, if the gas gauge on the dodge overestimated what was left in the tank or conditions on the road between here and Rockford were harsher than they anticipated, it could very easily mean the difference between life or death. Sure, it was a simple choice, but one loaded with risk. There was another issue they hadn't factored in. What about Evan? Would he be evacuated on his own? Would he head back home, uncertain where they'd all gone? Or would he stay at the plant, attempting to limit the damage? Or worse yet, could he have been killed in the blast? In good conscience, Nate couldn't simply leave his brother behind. He had already lost one sibling, he wasn't going to lose another.

Minutes later, everyone was assembled by the front door. Each of them had layered up in long johns, thick socks, sweaters along with all their outdoor winter gear. The go-bags Amy had helped them pack also contained essentials they would likely need in the coming days—dry socks, changes of underwear and clothing, along with a first-aid kit, iodine tablets, water bottle and some high-energy protein bars. It was important to be nimble in situations like this. Fight the urge to pack everything including the kitchen sink. Nor was it possible to anticipate any and every situation. Nate had read about how in special forces units, each member had their primary role and specialty. That helped them do more with less. Efficiency was the goal and Nate was glad he and Amy had insisted Evan's family had taken this seriously back when things were relatively calm.

Nate's own bag contained the majority of the high-tech gear he'd picked up over the years. Some of the items he'd found online while others had come from camping stores and specialty outlets. On the plus side, much of it was brand new and in working order.

While his family was prepared, he knew the vast majority of folks rarely thought further ahead than what to eat for dinner or watch on TV.

Then came the sound of a car horn from outside.

This wasn't time for democracy. It was time for a decision, and a decision he had already made. Confident they had most of what they would need, at least in the short term, he laid out the plan.

"We're going to load the pickup. Lauren, Hunter and Emmitt will ride with Carl and Liz in their car."

The horn sounded again and the boys looked outside at Carl and his wife waving them on.

"Where are we going?" Emmitt asked, frightened.

Nate swallowed and found his mouth had gone dry. "You'll be riding in evacuation buses organized by the town," he told them. "They're heading for Rockford."

Amy's coral-blue eyes flashed with surprise and then anger. "What do you mean 'you?' Aren't you coming with us?"

"I'll be right behind you," Nate said. "Following the convoy."

"And what about Evan?" Lauren asked, holding onto the straps of her bag as though it were a life preserver.

"After I drop you off at the bus, I'm going to swing by the plant and grab him." Nate could already hear his wife's protests before she spoke.

"Are you insane?" she shouted. "The whole town is filling with radiation."

"That's precisely why I'm dropping you off first. There's no way I want any of you exposed more than you need to be."

"Please don't leave my dad behind," Emmitt said, tears welling up.

Nate used both hands to pull his nephew's hat on tight. "No one'll be left behind, buddy. You have my word."

Outside, Carl and Liz's car honked again. Everyone hugged, before Lauren and the two boys headed out to meet them. Amy and Nate then filed into the garage where his truck sat waiting. While she got installed, he opened the sliding garage door manually. When he was done, he reached into his bag and pulled out the Geiger

101

counter. Switching it on, he took a single step outside and waved the device around once again. The readings were well above normal.

Moments later, with the Dodge idling in the driveway and the house locked up tight, the convoy left for Byron Middle School.

Chapter 19

Nate took the lead in the Dodge. The road ahead was marked by two parallel sets of tire tracks through the snow. Back and forth went the wipers as Amy fiddled with the vents to keep the windows from fogging up. He glanced down at the electronic gas gauge and saw he had sixty-five miles left in the tank. Of course, that was under ideal conditions, which these were certainly not. But with any luck, he would have more than enough fuel to get all of his family to safety.

An SUV before them slammed on its brakes for no apparent reason. Nate swerved, taking evasive action to avoid a collision.

"Whoa!" Amy cried, as she swayed in her seat, white-knuckling the drop-down grab handle.

"Looks like even the blind are out today," he said, grimacing.

Carl and the others were less than twenty feet behind them, taking advantage of the path Nate was plowing with the forward momentum of the truck.

He was about to express his surprise at how few cars were on Byron's streets when they turned onto the main thoroughfare. It was known as Highway 2 and among commoners as Blackhawk Drive and it wound through the core of the town like a long, slithering snake. Suddenly and out of nowhere, they were in bumper-to-bumper traffic.

"You have got to be kidding me," Nate shouted in disbelief. He thought of the Geiger again, and dared not pull it out lest it told him what he already knew. They were eating far more radiation than they should. He and Amy each swallowed a potassium iodide tablet. As he did so, he couldn't help thinking of Evan, over by the plant. There wasn't time for this. The traffic was going in one direction, northeast toward Rockford. It appeared a number of folks were going to take their chances. What they didn't know was that a pair of state troopers were going to escort the convoy of buses past this mess. Not everyone had a Carl and not every Carl had a shortwave, but Nate had both.

He spun the wheel and pulled out into the oncoming lane. Chunks of snow spun off his back tires.

"Babe, the hell are you doing?" Amy cried out, glaring at him as though he'd lost his mind.

With traffic flowing in a single direction, the real insanity, he had quickly realized, was waiting to be irradiated while sitting bumper to bumper. Nate drove out, passing the long line of cars. Carl was right behind him, along with a handful of others who had followed his lead.

"We don't have time for that parking lot," he told her and nudged the accelerator.

Whenever an oncoming car would approach, Nate would slow down, hug the line of cars on his right and let them pass. A few folks honked in protest as he went by, a heavy volume of snow splashing off his grill, but none of them knew the middle school was only his first stop in their evacuation plan.

"Up here at the light," Amy reminded him.

Now came the tricky part. Cutting across traffic in order to make the turn he needed. A cop directing traffic ordered the oncoming vehicles to stop. As soon as Nate reached the intersection, he spun the wheel, swinging his back tires out in a wide arc before regaining control. The stunned expressions on the faces of folks waiting in line was priceless. The cop too had to jump out of the way.

Still more amazing were the number of people in tiny hatchbacks in the distance, struggling to move forward. The source of the traffic jam he had narrowly avoided had quickly become clear. Half the cars were stuck in the snow. The rest were doing what they could to maneuver around the trapped vehicles. He wondered in that split second what would become of those who were stranded. There had to be dozens of them, all struggling in vain to dislodge their cars, woefully unprepared for the wintery hell that had descended upon them.

The middle school was not far from here and Nate powered down side roads blanketed deep with snow and not vehicles.

Moments later they came to a checkpoint. A sheriff's deputy patrol car was angled across the road. Nate pulled up and lowered his window.

"Only local traffic allowed," the officer told them. He was dressed in a long black coat and a matching knit cap, the latter pulled down over his ears. His cheeks were flushed from the cold.

"We're heading to the evacuation point," Nate said. He could just make out the school and the line of buses in the distance.

"No problem, sir. There's some nasty gridlock on Blackhawk Drive and we're trying to ensure folks aren't aiming to take shortcuts to avoid it."

"I understand." He pointed to the convoy idling by the school entrance. "We heard they're heading to Rockford. Can you confirm that?"

The deputy nodded. "Yes, sir. Rockford. Victory Sports Complex, to be precise. An indoor soccer pitch they've converted into a makeshift shelter. On a clear day, it couldn't be more than a twenty-minute drive, but I heard they're expecting the journey to take a good three hours. So you folks better get a move on. Seems those boys are itching to go."

Nate thanked him and pulled ahead. As they approached, more cars appeared. Many of them had taken the main avenues to get here, probably under the assumption the roads there would be less hazardous than the back streets. Nate sighed as their momentum slowed to a crawl. He wanted to honk, but didn't see the point.

Another deputy was in the school parking lot, trying in vain to direct traffic. The problem was, the townsfolk who were showing up in droves needed a place to park their vehicles. The police escort promised to the bus convoy had done a lot to sell the idea to anyone lucky enough to learn about it. Given the chaos, the town had barely begun the time-consuming task of informing people it was even an option. Surely, hundreds remained barricaded in their homes, some oblivious to the radiation sickness that would soon overtake them. A smaller, but more headstrong number likely knew of the danger, but refused to leave their homes for a wide variety of reasons ranging from protection of property to a not unreasonable concern that the situation outside might be more dangerous. They would take their chances with whatever nuclear fallout was coming their way. Nate certainly understood the impulse. More than a few residents had refused to leave New Orleans during Katrina until it was far too late. And even then, a surprising number had opted to go down with the ship rather than risk weeks or months away from home, sleeping in shelters.

Out of nowhere, another deputy appeared along the road and waved them into the parking lot. Nate waved as he passed, thankful these men hadn't abandoned their posts.

On the back of that, he couldn't help think about Evan. One could argue Evan was needed at the plant and that Nate should leave him be. Maybe earlier, when there had still been a chance of salvaging the situation. But not now, he told himself. Not after the worst-case scenario had come to pass.

The parking lot to their left would have been a nightmare had a team of pickup trucks with snowplows not cleared away at least some of the deep powder. It was a hack job, no doubt about it. But thankfully someone had had the foresight to see the logistical problems they would face as folks began showing up.

He spotted a natural depression between snow drifts just ahead and pulled the Dodge alongside it. With tires spinning, Carl pushed his snow-battered car ahead and parked in front of him. They got out into the numbing cold and began unloading. A man by the bus was shouting instructions to those beginning to board. "One bag only. Anything more will be left behind."

A guy with two giant suitcases was trying to argue his case without much success. Nate saw more people loaded like pack mules with backpacks, duffle bags and suitcases to boot. Nearby sat a graveyard of abandoned possessions cast aside in the snow. The sight was unnerving and only added to the growing sense that things in their small, once bucolic little town were unravelling at a rapid rate.

Lauren and the twins appeared next to them, each holding a single knapsack. By comparison to the hordes who appeared to have brought everything they owned, their little group looked vastly underprepared. But Nate and Amy understood, in a situation such as this, the quality of what you packed was far more important than quantity.

They headed toward the line of buses, Nate's heart seizing up with the thought of watching them step on board. Once he grabbed Evan, he would be right behind them. He knew that. But he couldn't shake the terrible feeling he wasn't going to see them again. The image of a bus overturning on the highway flashed before his eyes and he shoved it away. Given the crappy circumstances, this was the only choice that made sense. A traffic jam on the freeway could very well be a death trap. The police escort might just provide the edge they needed.

Nate hugged each family member in turn. "I'll be right behind you," he assured them. He reminded Amy how much he loved her. She rarely ever cried. It was one of the strange personality traits he loved about her. That was why the tears he saw threatening to roll over the lids of her eyes and down her cheeks struck him like a sharp blow to the solar plexus. She wasn't worried about meeting him in Rockford. What was upsetting her was that he was heading toward ground zero of a nuclear meltdown to get a man who might already be dead. But Evan wasn't just a man. He wasn't only a brother either. He was a husband and a father and Nate knew if they had packed up and fled town without him, he would never be able to live with himself.

Nate shook Carl's hand. "Look after them for me, will you?"

Carl nodded. "Sure thing." He held on for an extra second. "See you in Rockford."

One by one, Nate watched them board the first bus as others nearby continued to argue the policy on bag limits. The group sat toward the rear, close to the emergency exit. That was the smart play. If anything should go wrong, they could be the first ones out.

"Keep arguing all you want," the man shouted back. "We leave in thirty minutes with or without you."

Even though it wasn't directed at him, the warning got him moving nonetheless. He blew his wife a kiss and hurried back to the Dodge, distinctly aware that in more ways than one, time was quickly running out.

Chapter 20

Nate pressed his foot down on the accelerator, eager to close the two-mile distance between the middle school and the Byron nuclear plant as quickly as possible. The journey to retrieve his brother, however, was going far slower than he had hoped. Turned out he hadn't been the only one who thought cutting into oncoming traffic to beat the gridlock was a good, if not great, idea. Those with pickup trucks and SUVs had soon been followed by a whole range of vehicles ill-equipped for driving in such extreme conditions, among them sedans and sports cars. With the snow piling ever higher, his own truck was struggling to claw its way along. There was no wonder the roads were quickly becoming improvised junkyards.

Eventually, Nate reached the Rock River bridge, crossing over it and onto the narrow country road that led to the plant. He hadn't gotten more than fifty yards before he noticed conditions here were different than they were in town. For one, there were few, if any, vehicles. And the one or two he had seen were heading in the opposite direction. Which made sense, for only a fool would be venturing this way, toward the very danger which had caused people to flee town in the first place.

Here's looking at you, Nate.

His side of the road had been stamped with wheeled tracks from large vehicles. He remembered Evan explaining how the plant had been limping from one diesel delivery to the next, all in a futile attempt to keep the generators going. Could that account for the lack of snow on a country road?

The question was still front and center on Nate's mind when he glanced up over the tree line. There he spotted the same black cloud in the distance, looking like a giant bulbous demon standing out against the cold, grey sky. The fire at the plant was still burning. As he drew closer, he saw a handful of fire engines sitting idle, the firefighters themselves nowhere to be seen. Unlike firetrucks, engines carried within them seven hundred and fifty gallons of water. It appeared they had run dry without having much effect.

Gripping the wheel with one hand, Nate reached into his pocket and plucked out the Geiger counter. He spun the knob and listened as it crackled wildly to life. Every tiny sound felt like an irradiated dagger, piercing his flesh.

As the Dodge rolled toward the gate, two figures in orange radiation suits appeared and raised their weapons. Surely, Joe and Sam would recognize his truck. That was all Nate had time to think before the guards opened fire. Their rounds riddled his pickup, thudding into the engine block and tearing through the windshield. He slammed the brakes and flung himself over the center console, doing what he could to shield himself from the incoming fire. His truck drifted into a snowbank on the side of the road. Still hunched, Nate reached a hand over and gave the horn three long honks. The guards stopped shooting and began yelling for him to back up. Whoever these guys were, they weren't interested in chatting. So he threw the truck in reverse and hit the accelerator. The Dodge didn't respond, other than to begin spewing black smoke from beneath the hood. Soon it was filling the cab. He kicked open the driver's side door and came out with his hands raised. The two figures wearing inflatable suits approached. Behind them were two MRAP military vehicles.

This isn't Joe or Sam.

"Sir, this area is strictly off limits," the first one shouted, his voice distorted by the suit's built-in communication system. It felt like something out of a sci-fi movie.

"I'm looking for my brother," Nate began to explain. "Evan Bauer, is he here?"

"Sir, you can't be here."

"My brother," Nate shouted back. "I need to know where he is."

The two guards glanced at one another and lowered their weapons. The second man brought a handheld radio up to his face mask. He turned to Nate. "Evan Bauer, you said?"

Nate nodded, lowering his hands. He then fished the hat out of his pocket and pulled it down over his head to block out the cold wind biting at his cheeks. With the smoke from the engine thinning out, he popped the hood and waved the remaining black cloud away as he did his best to appraise the damage. It appeared the soldiers' bullets had shattered the radiator and water hose, among other things. His heart sank with the knowledge that they had effectively killed his only way home. Nate was stranded in the shadow of a nuclear plant in full meltdown.

Seconds later, one of the soldiers returned with some news. "A man named Evan Bauer was taken away by ambulance earlier this morning, but we have no further information."

Ambulance? The word struck him with the crushing force of a falling tree.

"What hospital?" he asked.

"I'm sorry, sir," said the first. "We don't have that information."

The second raised a hand. "For your own protection, I'm going to ask you to leave the area immediately."

"Really? In what?" Nate replied angrily, pointing at the Dodge, riddled with bullet holes. "You killed my truck and nearly me along with it."

"You didn't stop when we told you to."

That was a lie, but Nate wasn't in a position to debate the issue, not when his body was absorbing dangerous amounts of radiation. "Can you at least give me a lift back into town?"

"I'm afraid not."

Much like the billowing black cloud overhead, Nate felt a deep sense of despair settle over him. Not only because of his current situation—he knew now he had no hope in hell of reaching the convoy before it left— but also for the supplies in the truck bed he would be forced to leave behind. Packed there were containers with food and water they would likely need in the coming days and weeks, not to mention his weapons. And now most of that was gone on account of two guys with itchy trigger fingers.

Just then a glimmer of hope appeared when Nate spotted a firefighter, also in a radiation suit, wrestle his bulky frame behind the wheel of a fire engine. Maybe he could hitch a ride after all. Nate scrambled to grab vital items from the truck bed. He would have to leave most of the food and water behind. But not either of his pistols, nor the twelve-gauge and certainly not the ammunition that went with them. A shotgun without shells made a lousy club.

The fire engine approached the gate and stopped.

"I'll see if you can hitch a ride," the second guard said, approaching the driver. After a brief exchange, he turned and said, "He's heading back toward Byron. Says you can tag along. If I were you, I'd take the ride."

Stay and die of radiation poisoning or head back into town. It was hardly much of a choice. Nate climbed into the passenger side, depositing his go-bag, shotgun and an extra pack with food and water on the raised seats behind them. Nate barely had time to close the door before the fire engine tore off.

They were not on the road more than a minute before Nate said, "The military told me some of the plant workers were taken to the hospital."

The firefighter didn't bother to turn, since the bulky suit would have impeded his vision anyway. "Name's Denton," he said in a deep voice only slightly muffled by the suit. "Leon Denton, and I ain't never been so happy to leave a place in my entire life."

Leon was African-American with pronounced cheekbones and light brown skin. A guy like Leon would

114

stick out in a place like Byron, simply because most folks there were white, but Nate didn't remember ever seeing him around.

"What station you with?"

"Stillman Valley," Leon told him.

It was an even smaller town maybe a mile southeast of Byron, which explained why Nate didn't recognize him. "The guard said you were going to Byron."

"No, sir, I'm heading back to Stillman, I'm afraid."

"But Stillman's within the exclusion zone," Nate said, confused.

Leon nodded, his whole suit rolling with him. "That's why I'm dropping this here engine back where it belongs and then hightailing it to Chicago. Got family there and I'm sure they need some help getting on."

"You sure that's such a good idea, Leon?" Nate said, genuinely worried for the guy. "I mean, Chicago isn't exactly the safest place on the best of days."

Leon laughed. "Maybe for you, it's not."

Nate grinned and let it go. If this guy was determined to stick his head into a lion's mouth, who was Nate to try to stop him? Besides, saving family members had been a big part of the reason he was in this mess to begin with.

The truck bounced around as they plowed through snow drifts collecting on the road. "You mentioned before you'd never been so happy to leave a place. My younger brother was an engineer there. Evan Bauer. Do you remember anyone by that name?"

Leon squinted one eye for a moment. "Can't say I do." He grew silent after that. "Look, man, I don't want to worry you any more than you already are. I get you drove out in all this craziness looking for a loved one.

But there's something you should know, something you ain't gonna hear on the news even after the power comes back on. Only three people were taken out by ambulance. Twenty more were evacuated. Another thirty won't be found until spring when the snow melts. Wasn't no morgue we could take them to. We were stacking bodies up outside two and three deep. I can't say which group your brother was a part of. I only hope, for both your sakes, he was among the first two."

Nate listened with growing dread. The guards had told him his brother had been put on an ambulance. But soon after, they'd told him the fire engine was heading back to Byron. They had also claimed to have ordered him to stop before they fired. As hopeful as Nate was, the soldiers' track record for accuracy and truthfulness was not encouraging.

"I don't mean to worry you," Leon said, realizing he might have gone too far. "But I believe it's important to speak the truth. If you don't manage to find your brother at any of the local hospitals, you'll know where he is, back at the plant. In which case, it might also be said he was one of the lucky ones. To get out early, before the world goes and tears itself apart. Know what I mean?" He paused. "You a religious man, Mr. Nate?"

"Sure," Nate replied, without hesitation. "Are you?"

Leon nodded. "When all this started happening, I must admit, I couldn't help wondering whether humanity had been judged."

"Judged?"

Leon gripped the large steering wheel as they blasted through a fresh snow drift, jostling them in their seats. "That's right. Judged for our wicked ways by the

116

Almighty and found seriously wanting. Hard not to see the Lord's hand in all this."

Nate wasn't sure if it was the Lord's hand at work he saw or someone else's.

Up ahead was a split in the road. To the north was the bridge over the Rock River and Byron. To the east was the town of Stillman Valley.

"I'm gonna get out by the bridge," he told Leon. "I wanted to thank you for the ride. Not sure what I would have done."

Leon turned and flashed a toothy grin. "You woulda walked and probably not made it very far. I'm glad I could help, but I'm sorry I couldn't tell you more about your brother." He pulled the truck to a stop and Nate gathered his things. "Good luck finding him. And God bless."

The two men shook hands.

"Likewise to you, especially on your journey to the big city."

With that Nate exited the engine and began heading for the bridge into town. By now, his chances of reaching the convoy were zero. In all likelihood, it was on the highway, spiriting his family, and many other families, out of the immediate danger zone. Which only served to drive home the severity of his current predicament. He was outside in the numbing cold, without any proper food or shelter. Before him lay a journey—very possibly a journey on foot—to reach his family in Rockford. Add in the snow and the threat of radiation, peeling off layers of your life minute by minute, and what had seemed difficult before suddenly felt downright cataclysmic, maybe even impossible.

With the few possessions he owned slung over his shoulders, Nate tucked his head into the blowing snow and worked one foot in front of the other, all the while wondering if Leon had been right.

Chapter 21

The light was already beginning to fade by the time Nate reached a gas station on Blackhawk Drive. In spite of being in pretty good shape, his progress had still been rather pitiful. The snow was just too deep to maintain any kind of reasonable rhythm. Most Americans living above the fortieth parallel knew something about how harsh winters could be. But even they took for granted the thankless army of folks who often worked through the night to clear our streets and sidewalks after a big storm. Those brave or stupid enough to drive into this mess—a group he counted himself a part of—had by brute force removed some of the snow. Although in reality, it had been less snow removal and more snow displacement.

Already wiped from wrestling the sidewalk, his left knee throbbing something awful, Nate had quickly learned to stick to the road. The traffic he had passed earlier on his way to the middle school was now gone. In its place was the occasional car off on the side of the road, half buried and disappearing more and more with every passing minute. The vast majority weren't wrecks. They hadn't crashed. Their wheels simply had not been able to gain enough traction to move forward. In the pre-lights out world, driving a car in winter was perfectly all right. Throw the proper tires on and you could manage just fine. However, the rules were different now. The harsh conditions favored larger vehicles with four-wheel drive, though even that was no guarantee of success.

Slowly, deliberately, Nate weaved his way past one abandoned car after another. In spite of the cold, he could feel the sweat running down his back. His body had been running on adrenaline these last few hours. And as much as he didn't want to admit it, he was starting to come to terms with the fact that at some point he would need to stop and rest. Otherwise, he risked falling face first into the nearest snowbank and dying of hypothermia.

Eventually, he came to a Toyota Corolla, its rear lights glowing dimly beneath a layer of freshly laid snow. A thin trail of exhaust issued from the tailpipe for a moment before cutting off, along with the lights. Someone was still inside the car. Nate went to the driver's side window and cleared away the caked-on icy film gathering there. A woman's face stared back at him. She looked terrified, less by her situation and more by his sudden appearance.

"I won't hurt you," he assured her. "But you've got to leave town."

She shook her head, the ends of her blonde hair waving beneath her beanie. She looked somewhere in her late thirties with fairly pleasant features only slightly weathered by time and the normal ravages of life. "My boyfriend is coming to get me," she told him, her voice sounding muffled from behind her car window. "He's got a big ol' truck and will pull me out."

"How long have you been waiting?"

"Uh, a couple hours maybe. Piece of junk won't budge. I've been spinning the tires every few minutes but I ain't going nowhere."

Nate contemplated moving on, but how could he? Besides, the light was fading fast. "You spoke to him then?"

The woman shook her head. "Not exactly. I sent him a text." Her window was fogging up and she used her gloved hand to wipe a frisbee-sized hole.

Her answer filled Nate with a sinking feeling. "Your boyfriend might be looking for you, but I can almost guarantee he never got your text."

Her eyes narrowed, as though she suspected Nate was trying to pull a fast one. "Really? How can you be so sure?"

Nate's legs were cramping up from standing still. "You mind if I grab a seat for a minute? Rest up before I carry on?"

Her gaze shifted to the passenger seat next to her and then back to Nate. "I'm not sure. I don't know you."

"I've lived in Byron for near on fifteen years," he said, hoping that might change her mind.

The woman shook her head. "Sorry."

"All right," Nate said. "If he doesn't come soon, I suggest you get to Rockford any way you can. This whole town is being irradiated." And with that he turned

121

back to the road. He hadn't made it more than a half-dozen paces before she honked her horn.

When he turned back, her door was open and she was half out of the car.

"Okay, just for a minute, but don't try anything stupid. I have a gun."

"Good," Nate said out loud. Then to himself:

With everything that's happened, you're gonna need one.

•••

Nate settled his things in the narrow confines of the Corolla, removed his right glove and introduced himself.

"Jessie," she said, returning the gesture. "I'm not saying you're a psycho or anything, but you just can't be too careful. Know what I mean?"

Nate nodded, empty bottles clanking at his feet. "I can't blame you. Anyone with a depraved mind will see the lights go out and think he's in Disneyland."

"I noticed a micro-shift in your face when I introduced myself," she said. "Do we know each other?"

"A micro-what?"

She laughed. "It's hard to explain," she said, still grinning. The skin on her cheeks was pockmarked. "I tend to notice subtle things. Have since I was a little girl. Someone at work changes their hair and I'm the first to make note of it."

"I see. No, it's just that you look a bit like someone I knew."

Her features tensed. "Knew? Did something happen to her?"

"You could say that. It was a long time ago."

"Did she die?"

"No, one day she simply stepped off the face of the Earth," Nate said, appreciating the warmth, but wishing for a change of subject.

Jessie must have noticed another micro-shift in Nate's face or whatever she called it, because she changed the subject. "What are you doing out there all alone, Nate?"

"Heading to Rockford," he told her. "To my family."

"You didn't travel together?"

"It's kind of a long story." Nate reached into his bag and produced two power bars. He offered her one and she took it.

"Cheers."

"The least I could do to repay your hospitality." He took a bite and began the arduous task of chewing. That was the thing about power bars. They were loaded with protein and nutrients, but they could also give you lockjaw. He saw he wasn't the only one having a tough time.

"Got anything to drink in that magic bag of yours?" she asked.

Nate laughed. "It's far less magic than I would like it to be, but I sure do." He plucked out a bottle of water and handed it to her.

She smiled politely. "I was thinking about something a little harder."

Nate's gaze dropped to his boots and he suddenly realized the clanking sound he'd heard earlier was empty vodka bottles. "Nah, sadly nothing like that."

"Too bad. I don't have a drinking problem or anything, if that's what you're wondering."

123

Nate glanced over and saw her eyes were sharp and alert. She didn't look drunk, but that didn't mean she was happy about being sober. "Your life is none of my business, Jessie. You wanna drink, that's up to you."

"People get judgy, is all. That's why I worry sometimes."

"I can see why. But we both have larger things to worry about other than bad habits we can't seem to kick."

She seemed to agree with that.

"Listen," he said, closing his go-bag. "What will you do if your boyfriend doesn't show?"

"Oh, he'll show. Doogie can be a prick sometimes, but when push comes to shove he's always been there for me." She paused and studied him. "You a cop or something?"

Nate laughed. "I have that look, don't I?"

"Yeah, a bit," she said, sheepishly. "Well, maybe more than a bit. I'm right, aren't I?"

"I used to be a cop," he told her, as he rubbed at his throbbing knee.

"In Byron?"

"No, Chicago."

"Ouch, how was that?"

"Ouch is a pretty good way to put it. Was a big reason why we settled here in Byron. You see, my wife grew up on a farm and isn't a fan of big cities. She talked me into leaving, although it didn't take all that much to persuade me."

"You quit the force?"

Nate rubbed his gloved hands together, feeling the warmth slowly inching into the tips of his fingers. "I did."

"This may seem indelicate, but you ever killed anyone?"

He grinned. "No one who didn't deserve it."

Jessie's eyes flashed and Nate wasn't sure if it was fear he was seeing or something else. Talk of snuffing out a human life was turning her on. *Oh, boy.*

"Yeah, that's intense."

"Taking a life only requires squeezing a trigger. Living with what you've done, that can take a lifetime."

"No kidding. So you became a farmer, is that it?"

Jessie was a funny woman. "You ever think of becoming a reporter?"

She let out a bellowing laugh. "Way back in high school I had a nickname—Snoopy, you know, like the dog? But also because I like to ask a lot of questions. So, Mr. Ex-Cop, what do you do now? Or should I say, what *did* you do?"

"Worked security at the power plant for a while," he began.

"The one that just blew up?"

"The very same. If my bosses had listened, there's a chance, slim as it might be, that Byron wouldn't be facing this mess. At least not on this scale."

"So you know what happened?" she asked, her brow furrowing. "You'd think we'd lose power after it blew, not before. I find the whole thing rather confusing, to be honest."

"We were hacked," he said, deciding he would come right out and tell her. There was no point in keeping it a

125

secret, even if knowing couldn't change the danger they were facing. "My brother was an engineer there, one of the heroes who tried to keep the core from melting down. Whoever did this didn't only want to cripple the country. They wanted to utterly destroy us."

Marie—Jessie, her name was Jessie—stared at him, not saying a word. Then: "Well, they sure did a bang-up job."

"I know, it's pretty crazy," he went on. "Nuclear power plants are among the most secure facilities in the world. In part because they're completely cut off from the internet. Hackers have no way in. Well, that was what the people who ran the plant thought. They're a publicly traded company, you know. Out to make a profit. So when I started pushing reforms, I think they worried any word of vulnerabilities would crater their stock price."

"So they did nothing."

Nate arched an eyebrow. "Not exactly nothing. They fired me and enforced a clause in my contract that prevented me from telling anyone what I knew. What happened was totally avoidable. But I'd be lying if I told you it hadn't happened elsewhere."

"Other plants have had meltdowns?" Her eyes were wide now.

"I've heard more than a few nuclear plants have suffered the same fate, but not all of them."

"For some reason I'm not feeling very reassured by that."

"This was a sophisticated attack, perhaps the most sophisticated in history. Power plants were not the only ones hit. If you caught the news the evening before the lights went out, personal bank and investment accounts were also wiped. We're talking trillions of dollars. Assuming we manage to claw our way out of this mess, the economy may never recover."

"I need a drink," she said, her face ashen. He handed her the disposable water bottle and she shook her head. "Oh, no, not that kinda drink. You know that old saying about ignorance being bliss? Well, I think whoever came up with that little beauty sure nailed it."

"What about you?" he asked, deciding a change of subject was in order. "You work somewhere in Byron?"

"Sure, I waitress part-time at the diner on 2nd and Maple."

"I know the place," Nate said. "Never been there though. Any good?"

"The food or the work?"

"Hmm, both."

"I paid part of my way through college by working at a carwash in the summers" Nate told her. "You might not be running around like a server at a restaurant, but cleaning a car inside and out on a sweltering summer day can be brutal in its own way." And for a moment, Nate caught the smell of asphalt growing soft in the sun's searing rays. The sound of the radio by the register belting out songs over a warm current of air. These memories weren't merely distant, they were from a world Nate was beginning to think he might never see again.

Chapter 22

Nate's eyes opened in a dark and unfamiliar place. For a moment, he wondered where he was. Back home in his bed, lying next to Amy? He reached over and felt someone next to him. But then the angles were all wrong, so were the smells. The odor of vodka wafted up at him. Finally, he reached a hand into his pocket, came out with his phone and switched on the flashlight.

The glow illuminated the interior of the Corolla. Snow covered the windshield, blotting the world outside from view. Jessie was there, fast asleep, her head resting on his shoulder. He went back to his phone. The time stamp at the top of the screen read eight o'clock. There were no messages nor any reception bars. His battery life was at fifty-one percent. As reality flooded back in, it left a searing pain in his chest, the same one he felt whenever he thought about memories of home, of the life he had built with Amy. An agony made worse whenever he skimmed through the many photos he kept on his phone. Those images were beckoning him. Encouraging him to put one foot in front of another.

Get up and keep moving, Nate.

It was that voice again. A firm reminder that he couldn't sleep, not now, not here. He'd only stopped for a momentary rest from the cold and the wind and the way the impossibly deep snow made his knee ache.

He peeled open the door with a snap and a creak and saw that it was light outside. Not daytime light, but the kind that was common in winter when the streets seemed to take on a hazy glow.

Outside, the wind might have let up a little, but not the snow. That still fell in earnest, large flakes tumbling sideways across his field of view.

"What time is it?" Jessie asked, her voice sleepy.

"Eight," he replied.

"In the morning?"

"No, at night. We fell asleep for about an hour or so."

She sat up and rubbed at her eyes. "Got any more of that water?"

He handed her what was left in the disposable bottle. "All yours. Listen, I'm gonna head out. You're welcome to join me. I know I don't need to tell you it isn't safe to stay here."

"I don't think I should leave," she said, genuinely sad.

Nate watched her for a silent moment, wondering whether he should circle around, fling open her door and drag her out for her own good. Doogie wasn't coming. Nate knew that. The woman was clinging to a fantasy.

Someone wiser than him once said, "You can lead a horse to water, but you can't make it leave a radioactive exclusion zone." He decided to ask her one final time.

"Thank you," Jessie replied, her voice firm. "But I'm going to keep waiting. Maybe we'll see you in Rockford. You can introduce me to your family."

He told her that would be nice and to take care of herself. And with that Nate grabbed his things and stepped out into the stinging cold. In spite of the cramped confines of the sedan, his knee was already feeling much better. He was no more than a few yards out when he turned to see she was outside, clearing the snow off her windscreen. She stopped and waved one last time. Nate did the same, still uncertain whether she was being incredibly brave or downright foolish.

It wasn't long before Jessie was out of sight. Ahead of him, Nate caught the flash winking off a reflective street sign. He spun and spotted a pair of headlights heading his way. He hadn't seen another working vehicle since his ill-fated journey to the plant to grab Evan. Moving off the road—the sidewalks were downright impassable—Nate stuck out his thumb and wore the kind of smile that would make a flight attendant green with envy.

The lights got closer and Nate could see it was a Tiguan, fighting through the chop. The vehicle slowed as it drew even with him and then sped past.

"Jerk," Nate called out. He'd gotten a good glance inside as it went by. The thing was empty, apart from the driver.

The thought crossed his mind that maybe seeing the shotgun slung over his shoulder was giving people pause. He switched it to the other shoulder and carried on. Ten minutes later, he was further down the road when he spotted another pair of headlights. As he had done before, Nate moved off the road, slid the shotgun out of view, and stuck out his thumb. This time, the truck never even bothered to slow down.

He sighed. It appeared the 'every man, woman and child for themselves' rule was already in full effect.

Slogging along as he was, at times through powdery, freshly fallen snow and at other times through harder, wind-packed stuff, was making for slow going. If he'd gone beyond three hundred meters in the last hour, it would be a surprise to him. The tips of his fingers and toes were starting to feel numb. Strangely, his core felt like it was overheating from the exertion.

Or am I suffering from radiation poisoning?

He unzipped the top of his jacket, watching the steam escape. That was water his body was losing. Liquid he would need to replace sooner rather than later.

One hour passed before Nate reached the intersection, the one where earlier in the day he had cut across oncoming traffic, fishtailing into the backroads that led to Byron Middle School. He paused for a moment, working to catch his breath and sort out what do to next.

If he continued straight, Blackhawk Drive would eventually become Highway 2, the road that led to Rockford. The stretch between the two cities was about fifteen miles. Far too long to complete in a single hike, bum knee or not. Such a trek in July would have been child's play. Armed as he was, Nate would have gone as long as he could. Light to see by might have been a problem, but walking out beneath the stars on a warm summer night? Heck, it almost had an inviting ring to it.

Attempting the same thing now was liable to end with a man frozen to death somewhere along the shoulder of Highway 2. He did not have the slightest clue how to build an igloo or even a snow shelter for that matter. If there was no car he could break into along the way, the chances were good he would simply freeze to death.

As if to drive home the point, Nate spotted a dark boot sticking out of a nearby snow pile. He hurried over to it—of course, hurry was a relative term nowadays—and dug into six inches of powdery accumulation. With each swipe, a prone human form was coming into view. It was a man in a dark pair of blue jeans. His sneakers were black and looked battered, but expensive. Nate freed his upper body and then his head. He was dead, probably had been for hours. He cleared away the final bits around his face. This wasn't a man at all. It was a boy, no older than thirteen or fourteen. A pair of AirPods were seated firmly, and maybe permanently, into his ears. No more than a couple of years separated him from Hunter and Emmitt. What had he been doing out here alone? Why had he lain down in the snow, never to rise again? Exhaustion?

Keep moving, Nate.

He had started hearing that voice more and more these last couple of days. That part of him determined to survive appeared to be chiming in every once in a while with a mental slap across the face. Nate's gloves and hat were wet and caked with snow and yet this dead kid before him was dressed for Siberia. He was wearing a fur-lined aviator hat along with a pair of plush mittens. It seemed a pity to let them waste away on a corpse, however young that corpse might be. And yet the act of stripping a dead body also seemed grotesque and reprehensible.

Don't be silly. Take the stuff. You'll need it.

Nate stared at the young boy's face, his youthful, innocent features frozen into something resembling a sneer. He'd read an article recently about dead climbers on Mount Everest and how their bodies acted as macabre landmarks for those on their way up. "Hang a right at Green Boots, and then a left at Yellow Jacket." Back when things were normal, the notion had seemed rather sick to him, but many of those bodies had been sitting in Everest's deep-freeze for decades. It was not practical or safe to chop them out of the ice and bring them down. They were part of the mountain now. A piece of the landscape. This kid felt much the same. No one but family was going to move him. Here he would lie until spring and summer when Mother Nature would complete the process.

Again came that gently commanding voice.

Nate swore before grabbing the hat. When that was done, he took the mitts as well.

He didn't recall any religious passages condemning stealing from the dead. If the devil wanted him, he would have to wait. Nate wasn't ready to die. Not just yet. He had too much to live for.

Like descending from the summit of Everest, Nate knew the journey back to his family would be arduous and brimming with danger, both natural and man-made. And like that same great mountain, the dead and dying would mark his path, a string of twisted landmarks on the way out of hell.

Chapter 23

After knocking the ice off his new hat and mitts, Nate contemplated what direction to go in. Heading straight, along Highway 2, would begin the long and difficult trek to Rockford. To the right was the side road that led to the middle school. Going that way would add time, no doubt about it. On the flipside, he would eventually reach the school itself, where he could take shelter and rest. The route along the highway snaked in tandem with Rock River and offered nowhere he could hole up to refuel his body and recharge his spirits.

Right it is then.

Thus far that little voice hadn't led him astray. And so he was busy putting one foot—albeit awkwardly—in front of another when he realized heading toward the school offered him another advantage. If somehow, the bus convoy hadn't yet left—doubtful as that was—or became stuck in the snow and forced to return, then there was a chance he might find them there. Without any way of communicating, him setting off for Rockford when his family had never left Byron would quickly start to feel like a sick comedy of errors. How we'd ever lived without cell phones, Nate did not know.

The backstreets to the middle school were lined with homes typical of the area, somewhere between country and suburban. Bungalows were plentiful, with generous yards on both sides. It was hard to tell how many of these homes were occupied. The town, with the county's help, had begun the impossible task of telling folks to evacuate. This area was still seven miles inside the exclusion zone. That meant depending on the direction of the wind, everything here could be contaminated, including Nate. Contrary to popular belief, exposure to radiation didn't guarantee immediate death or even cancer. Genetics had a part to play as well. Some near Fukushima and Chernobyl had got sick and died from the same exposure that had little to no effect on others.

Nate made a point of walking inside the tire tracks on the road. It was hard going, and more than once he lost his balance or his tired legs gave out, sending him tumbling into a cloud of snow. That was when he recalled the young boy at the intersection, imagining that must have been the way things had gone for him. He had fallen down and never found the will to get back up. Perhaps that was the difference between them. Nate had something to live for. Two things, actually, if you counted his unborn daughter.

By the time he reached Byron Middle School, the building stood darkly silhouetted against a distant bank of angry storm clouds. The snow wasn't letting up and, judging from what he saw on the horizon, might not for a while to come. Nate's next observation had to do with the cars out front. Many were parked haphazardly, in pretty much the same way their terrified owners had left them earlier in the day. But cars was all he saw. Not a truck among them. At least the folks who had made it to the school realized they wouldn't get much further. The buses were gone too and Nate couldn't help feeling a prick of disappointment. Expectation and anticipation were two different, yet related emotions. He'd known they would be gone, but even so, the letdown was hard to deny.

His knee was also starting to act up again, helped in no small amount by the cold. The numbness that had settled back in shortly after parting company with Jessie had gradually crept along each of his appendages. His nose and cheeks had taken most of the beating, buffeted almost constantly by the glacial wind. Little by little, the once simple act of putting one foot in front of the other was becoming harder than passing a breathalyzer on New Year's Eve.

Nate reached the front door and found it locked.

Really?

Who locked a school in an exclusion zone? Every moment he spent outside was definitely more dangerous than standing between four solid walls. He needed somewhere relatively warm so he could eat, drink and be merry, as they said—if by merry they meant sleep. Knocking on doors in the neighborhood or, worse than that, breaking into someone's vacant home was the last thing Nate wanted to do. He had recently been on the receiving end of just such an act and had come inches away from killing at least one of the thieves. The idea of turning any further toward that dark side was out of the question. If a window needed to be broken, it would belong to the school district.

He swung around to the side entrance, tried the door and hit another dead end.

Strike two!

For reasons unknown, when the school had been built back in the late eighties, the county architect had laid out the structure in the shape of the letter H. That meant five entry points if you counted the one out front and courtyards on both the east and west sides. So far, he had struck out on the first two. That left three more.

Nate was on his way to the door at the end of the western wing when something in the courtyard caught his eye. The make and model was not clear, but the fact that it was a pickup truck was obvious, even though the thing was covered in about eighteen inches of snow. The driver's side door was open too, ever so slightly, and the truck seemed to be leaning forward. The hint of tire tracks led from the road to the truck's location, which immediately lit up the cop part of Nate's brain. Not because he thought a crime was necessarily in progress. If someone wanted to snatch boxes of number two pencils and reams of lined paper, they could be his guest. It told him the truck had arrived after the storm had already been raging for most of the night. In the few hours since they'd been abandoned, the cars in the parking lot had collected no more than six to eight inches.

This beauty could be his ticket out of here.

He drew closer and noticed the now amorphous shape of several sets of footprints in and around the truck. Nate batted around some of the snow near the driver's side door and pulled it open. Using the light from his phone, he first noticed the steering wheel, emblazoned with the Chevy symbol. Next to come into view was a charging cord for an iPad, which trailed out from the USB port in the center console. The iPad itself was gone. But he did see something else. In a spot where the upholstery had once been beige now sat a deep crimson bloodstain. The flesh along the back of Nate's neck was beginning to tingle something fierce. He closed the door and withdrew his pistol as he circled around the vehicle. The fuel cap was dangling by the truck's side.

Has someone syphoned the gas?

The snow was deep around the truck, enveloping it in a sort of cocoon which, undisturbed, would last through the coldest months. Up near the front, he knocked loose powder from the passenger door and saw holes, bullet holes. Other signs of a gun battle soon came out from hiding: two in the side window and another in the front right tire. The thing was flat now and Nate couldn't help feeling some of the air go out of him as well. There was no longer any room for doubt, this was Lauren's truck, the one those thugs had stolen earlier. It had also become clear that more than one of Nate's rounds had landed, in turn wounding the driver and puncturing the front tire. But how could a man keep driving with a hole in his side and one in his front tire? The answer, he supposed, was easy enough: adrenaline. The miracle drug—technically a hormone—that our bodies produced had the capacity to push us to nearly unbelievable feats of strength and endurance. Maybe other, synthetic drugs had also been at play. As far as Nate was concerned, you had to be morally dead, mentally unhinged or on something to start stealing only hours into a major power outage. Maybe a touch of all three.

The vague outline of foot traffic, only partly filled in, led from the truck to an inner courtroom door Nate hadn't seen. The door looked like it had been kicked open. On a hunch, he brushed at the snow on the ground next to the boot prints and saw splotches of blood.

With his pistol in one hand and the flashlight from his phone in the other, Nate headed inside.

Chapter 24

Nate's footfalls echoed on that hard, industrial flooring common to just about every civic building in the country. The school was dark. His hands were in the closest approximation to the Harries technique he could muster. Harries normally meant wrapping the weak hand with the flashlight under the hand holding the gun. It had been around since the 70s, but Nate was sure no one had ever used the technique with a cell phone light.

Pools of shadow vanished as he swung from left to right. He was in a corridor and coming to a t-intersection. Even looking forward, he couldn't help seeing the trail of blood. Nate drew on his training as he slowly and methodically made his way past classrooms and lockers.

At the end of this blood trail was the thief who had stolen from them. Eagerly, he followed it down a flight of stairs. The droplets were large and bulbous, thickening around the outer edges. A slight film forming over the top. That told him the thug who had come this way had done so more than a few hours ago.

Nate passed more classrooms along with a teacher's lounge, all of them eerily silent and devoid of life. Planting his feet, he aimed the light at the floor up ahead. The trail of blood led to a nearby room with a set of double doors, both of which stood ajar.

Heel to toe, Nate crept along in that direction, lowering the light as he drew closer. When he was a few feet away, he used a maneuver called cutting the corner. This meant angling into the room while at the same time limiting his own exposure to enemy fire. The blood led into a wide-open space that swallowed up most of the diffuse light from his phone. He noticed painted lines over the wooden floor. This wasn't a cafeteria. It was a gym.

On the bleachers in the distance lay a figure in a grey winter jacket and dark baggy pants. Pooling beneath him was a dull liquid that looked from here like motor oil, but Nate knew better. The figure moved ever so slightly. This was no corpse he had stumbled upon. Corpses couldn't shoot back, but even wounded men could be dangerous.

Nate put up his pistol, unslung his shotgun and pushed into the gymnasium's ink-black darkness. You can't hold a flashlight and use a shotgun at the same time, so Nate slid the phone into one of the front pockets of his jacket and pulled the zipper as tight as it would go, synching it in place. Where he turned, so too would the light, no matter how feeble it was at illuminating such a wide-open space.

He staggered toward the figure, wincing with every torturous footstep. By now the ache was no longer in his trick knee. Every bone in his body seemed to be crying out in protest, begging for him to find a safe, quiet place where he could lie down and replenish. Swinging to his left, Nate noticed items strewn about the floor. Bags of chips, stacks of canned food and cases of Bud Light. It was as though someone had gone on the mother of all shopping sprees only to dump their spoils in a heap. But maybe heap was the wrong word. Scanning the items, it was starting to look less like heaping and more like stockpiling.

A sound came out of the darkness to his right. He turned and froze when he spotted a pair of silvery eyes glaring back at him. The unsettling orbs were housed in a large cage, the kind people used on planes to transport pets. Was it a fox? he wondered. No, it was far too big. A stray dog maybe? There was a feral, menacing look in those eyes.

The two stared at one another, unblinking, for what felt like an eternity.

You don't belong here, that look said.

And Nate could not have agreed more.

If the dog had surprised him, what he witnessed in a cage barely ten feet from the first truly knocked the breath from his lungs. A girl, no more than fifteen years old, curled into a ball, sleeping. She had black, matted hair tucked under a bright red winter hat.

Each of the cages was secured with a heavy padlock. He swung back to the wounded man on the bench, who was reaching out with a single, bloody hand. Nate racked the shotgun and centered the barrel at his chest. A pistol sat on the floor next to him. It was a Beretta 9mm. Nate bent down, scooped it up and slid it into his jacket pocket.

"I need water," the wounded guy said in a barely audible whisper.

This guy was beyond caring about warding off intruders. Had Nate put a gun in his hand, he probably wouldn't have had the strength to pull the trigger.

Ignoring his pleas, Nate shouldered the shotgun and began rifling through his pockets. "Where's the key, you sick son of a bitch?"

"Water, man. I need water." His skin was pale. The blood from his wounded abdomen had saturated his clothing. The thugs he might have once called friends had not even bothered to clean or dress the bullet hole, let alone attempt to stop the bleeding. Dead man walking, that was what he was. They were no better than that wild animal they had put in a cage.

"This hole in your gut was my gift to you, for stealing our truck."

The man's sallow eyes widened.

Nate found keys in the front pocket of the guy's jeans at about the same time he caught the raucous sound of people approaching. They were practically around the corner. Nate tossed the keys to the girl, who was now sitting up. They skidded along the laminated gym floor, clanging as they struck the front of her cage. She grabbed and worked them up the bars and toward the padlock.

Nate then swung the shotgun off his shoulder and spun.

"Drop it or you're dead," a gruff voice called out.

Standing before him were two men. The first stood with his feet firmly planted, gripping an assault rifle. He was a giant of a man, six four, wearing a duster jacket

143

and heavy work boots. Although most of his face was covered in shadow, Nate could make out just enough detail to tell the guy was an ugly SOB. And judging from his height and confidence, he was probably also the leader of this upstart band of thieves.

Before Nate could get a good look at the other thief, he disappeared into a patch of darkness. Any way you sliced it, Nate was at a serious tactical disadvantage. He was out of the effective kill range of his weapon. With luck, he might pepper one of the thugs, but the other would surely get him before he had time to take a second shot. It also didn't help the two had split up with one hiding in darkness.

"Gabby, you got sights on this guy?" the tall ugly one asked his buddy.

"Sure do, Jack," came the disembodied reply.

Ugly grinned. "This is your last chance before my friend here puts you out of your misery."

"I've seen how you take care of your friends." Nate raised the shotgun in the air with one hand. "If I drop this, I have your word you'll let me go?"

Ugly held up three fingers. "Scout's honor."

Nate knew he was lying, but set the shotgun down. It wouldn't do him much good anyway.

"We good?"

"He's got my piece," the wounded man called out.

"Everything," Ugly shouted, referring to any weapons Nate was hiding. "Or there's no deal."

Nate sighed, removing the 9mm, holding it in the air with two fingers.

"What about now?"

Gabby emerged from the darkness with a Glock 21. He reached to snatch the pistol from Nate's outstretched hand and that was when Nate dropped the gun and lunged. For a split second, Gabby's eyes traced the falling weapon. Nate's focus was squarely on the weapon in Gabby's other hand. In one motion, he grabbed and twisted it back and out of the man's grip and into his own. Gabby's cheeks flared out with anger as he struggled in vain to regain possession.

Seeing what was happening, Ugly leveled his semi-automatic and began firing, following Nate as he rolled out of the way. Ugly's rounds tore up the wooden bleachers, thudding into the wounded guy and then into Gabby. Nate began firing back while in mid-roll, aiming for center mass as he'd been taught. Head shots were for movies, video games and anyone who had never been in a real firefight.

One of his rounds struck Ugly's left leg, another tore open his right bicep. The rifle fell from the thief's grip and clattered to the floor. Nate squeezed the trigger to finish him off and heard a click. He looked at his pistol and saw the slide was all the way back.

Ugly noticed too and pulled back his duster. He was going for a secondary weapon.

Nate had one too, his Sig, tucked into the concealed-carry belt holster. The question was, who would draw first?

Ugly was in the process of raising his pistol when a blur leapt through the air and sank its teeth into his wrist. Ugly screamed in agony, trying desperately to wrench his hand free from the animal's vicious jaws. Nate took that opportunity to close the distance and put two in Ugly's chest.

The thief slumped forward dead. The dog disengaged and stood watching Nate, its maw smeared with blood. But this wasn't a dog, was it? The thing was too large, its grey fur tinged with patches of light and dark. The charcoal-colored pattern around its eyes was particularly striking. It looked like a mask. A family pet this was not. Nate was staring back at a full-fledged wolf and it was coming this way.

To his left was the young girl who also stood staring at him.

"Can you tell your wolf to back down?" Nate said. It was a beautiful, majestic beast, but if it came at him or showed the slightest hint of aggression, he would drop it without hesitation.

The girl smiled nonchalantly, scooping up the 9mm Nate had dropped on the floor. "He isn't mine."

The wolf's attention was suddenly diverted by something Nate could not hear or see. A second later, a fat guy stepped into the gym, pushing a dolly stacked with cases of Coors beer. He stopped so suddenly the top cases rolled off and onto the floor with a loud thud. A handful of cans burst. Foamy beer leaked out from the thin cardboard cases.

"What the...?" he stammered, his enormous jowls quivering with stunned surprise.

The wolf was facing him now, a growl emanating from the back of its throat, low and threatening.

The fat man swore and tore off as fast as his meaty legs could carry him. The wolf gave chase.

And judging by the blood-curdling screams which quickly followed, it was safe to say he didn't get very far.

146

Chapter 25

In spite of what had gone down in the school's gymnasium, Nate was in no hurry to rush back out into all that cold and thigh-deep snow.

Searching the bodies, distasteful as that was, had proven useful. Among the spoils was Ugly's AR, Gabby's Glock 21 and a box of rounds for each of them. A couple cans of Bud Light couldn't hurt either, nor could a bag of Doritos and some canned corn and beans.

He turned to the young girl and tossed a can of tuna her way. She fumbled and nearly missed it in the low light.

"Thanks," she said, heading over to Ugly's body and peeling the knapsack off his back. Rather than going through it item by item, the girl turned it upside down and gave it three or four good shakes. A clump of socks, underwear and porno mags came spilling onto the floor.

"Eww," she said, kicking them aside. She then began collecting items of her own, stuffing them into her new bag.

Nate set aside the AR, held out his hand and properly introduced himself.

"Dakota," the girl said, shaking back.

"That's quite a grip you've got."

She smiled sheepishly. "I get it from my dad, I guess. He was known for his hard shakes."

"I have to admit," Nate said, "you're the first girl I've ever rescued from a cage."

"That's too bad. How did it feel?"

Nate paused to think. "Pretty necessary. I mean, I felt bad enough finding that wolf locked up. Speaking of which…" He grew quiet and heard nothing, apart from the sound of his own breathing. Had the beast left or was it still around? he wondered.

"If he has any sense," she said, "he'll find a way out and head back into the wild where he belongs."

She was right, but Nate would keep his weapons handy all the same. "Where are your folks?" he asked.

The corner of Dakota's mouth twisted into an expression somewhere between sadness and anger.

"I see. Well, listen, I need to rest a couple hours. Either way, we should get out of this gym before any more of Ugly's men come back."

"The four we killed were the only ones I ever saw."

For the record, Ugly had killed two of his own men, Nate had got one and the wolf had finished off the last. But what did details like that matter at a time like this, right?

"How about we find a spot on the other side of the building?" Dakota suggested. "Give you a chance to rest your old-man legs."

Nate wasn't sure whether to laugh or be offended. "These old-man legs just helped you out of a cage."

"I didn't mean it in a bad way," she said, and he could tell she was being honest. To most teenagers, anyone beyond their mid-twenties was practically a senior citizen.

"No harm done," Nate said. "What do you say we head out?"

She agreed.

Nate led them past Ugly's corpse—splayed by the double doors—and then along a darkened corridor brimming with shadow. Lockers ran along both sides of the wall, punctuated by the occasional classroom. They soon found themselves at the front of the school where Nate had encountered the locked doors. He pointed to a room with the words 'Principal's Office' stenciled on the door.

"Oh, great!" Dakota moaned. "The world's coming to an end and I'm still being sent to the principal's office."

Nate smiled. "You're not the studious type, I take it."

"Not for boring things, no."

He let that one go, too. Nate kept the AR in the low ready position as he swept the reception area followed by both offices. The one on the left was the principal's. The other belonged to the vice. One had to pass the reception area to reach the offices. That gave them two layers of defense, much like a castle with concentric

149

walls, two or more curtains of fortification an attacker would need to defeat in order to get inside.

With Dakota's help, they barricaded the main door by stacking furniture against it. When they were done, he waved a hand to the office on the right. "Madam Vice Principal," he said, ushering her inside.

She entered laughing, but didn't close the door.

Nate took the principal's office. There wasn't a couch. That was his first observation. As a consolation prize, he found a plush leather chair behind a large oak desk. He dropped his bag, set the AR against a bookshelf and fell into the seat. A tiny blast of air hissed out from under his weight. He pulled at the metal release and reclined, propping his feet on the desk. Nate basked in the warm glow born of simple pleasures. Within ten seconds, he was fast asleep.

Chapter 26

Day 4

Nate came awake to the sound of giggling. Early morning light streamed in through the windows. Slowly the room came into focus. A young girl was standing at the doorway, bent over, covering her mouth.

"What's wrong? Are you sick?"

She shook her head, her thin body twitching. "I'm not sick, I'm laughing."

"Oh, well, what's so funny then?"

Dakota straightened and leaned against the wall, the traces of a smirk still on her face. "You snore. Did you know that?"

"That right?" Nate said, shrugging. He remembered Amy mentioning something about snoring one or two million times.

The young girl folded her arms. "Well, as snoring goes, you're the GOAT."

"The what?" He sat upright.

"Greatest of All Time. GOAT. I'm not making fun of you. It's a compliment."

"Doesn't sound like one. Did I wake you up?"

Her left eyebrow rose. "Me? Hell no. I sleep like a corpse. Can sleep anywhere at anytime. It's one of my gifts."

He recalled finding her in that cage, curled up in a ball sleeping. "I've never heard someone call sleeping a talent," Nate said. "But I give you points for creativity."

"Fake it till you make it, right?"

That one made him laugh.

"Hungry?" she asked.

"Famished."

"Good," she replied, smiling. "I made breakfast."

"Really?" Nate was impressed.

She handed him a can of beans, a fork sticking out the top. "I would have made eggs and bacon, if we had either of those things and a stove to cook it on. I make a mean Egg McMuffin, I'll have you know."

Nate scooped some beans into his mouth. "Stop teasing me. Right now, I'd run naked through the snow for an Egg McMuffin."

Dakota beamed with a devilish smile. "And I'll film it and put it on YouTube. 'Naked Old Guy Versus Winter.' A million hits guaranteed." She clamped a hand over her mouth. "Oops, sorry. I said the O word."

Nate fought a smile. "I just love how you think people my age have one foot in the grave. But I guess I shouldn't complain. There was a time I was the same way." He waved his fork at her. "How old are you anyway?"

"Fifteen," she said.

"Huh, hope you don't mind me saying, but I took you for younger than that."

She nodded. "I get that a lot. I'm skinny, that's probably why. I have a fast metabolism, what can I do?"

"When I was your age, I was desperate to hit eighteen, then twenty-one, then twenty-five. Growing up seemed to take forever. Far as I was concerned, the days couldn't fly off the calendar fast enough. But the older you get, the faster time seemed to speed by. Call it nature's cruel joke. Not much you can do about it, except focus on making sure tomorrow is better than today."

Her expression darkened. "Yeah, well, none of that matters anymore."

Nate returned to his beans. "How'd you get these cans open, by the way?"

"With this," she said, producing a multi-tool from her pocket.

"You find that on one of the dead guys?"

She shook her head, her black straight hair dancing about her shoulders. "This one's mine. I got something different off them."

"What's that?"

She nudged her tiny chin in his direction. "That fork you're using."

Nate looked down at it and couldn't help but laugh. Normally the thought might have turned his stomach, but hunger had a funny way of making the things that used to feel important suddenly insignificant and maybe even petty. That grounding thought drew his attention back to matters more serious.

"Where were you going when they grabbed you?" he asked.

"I was halfway from Leaf River," she explained—a pinprick of a town a few miles west of Byron. "Heading to my uncle Roger's place."

Nate had mentioned her folks earlier and that hadn't exactly elicited a positive response, but he felt it was important to find out where this girl belonged. "Why your uncle? Are your parents still around?" He really meant 'alive,' but wasn't certain how to frame such a delicate question.

She shrugged. "I'm not sure where they are. My dad started a dog-walking business over the internet that blew up and made us rich. My mother was a real-estate agent, one of the best ones in the country."

"So far that all sounds like good stuff to me."

"Maybe on the surface it does. But both of them are about as self-absorbed as you can imagine. I used to live with them in a penthouse apartment in Chicago. We had drivers and servants. That is, until they sent me away to live with my uncle. And then when that didn't work out they bought me an apartment in Leaf River."

"Your own apartment at fifteen?" Nate asked, shocked. "Is that even legal?"

"It is when you have the right connections."

"Must have been hard going from the big city to a place the size of Leaf River. It's so tiny, it makes Byron feel like a thriving metropolis."

Dakota sneered. "No kidding. They always liked to keep me at arm's length. Far enough that I wouldn't be seen, but close enough that they could whip me back if the Feds ever found out."

"I've never heard anything like that," Nate said, and he meant it. If that was truly the case then it made sense why she would be heading to find her uncle. "This uncle of yours, what's his name?"

"Roger. But he usually calls himself something else. Ranger or something like that."

"Ranger? Okay. Is he from Byron?"

Dakota shook her head. "Roger has two places. A house in Rockford and a cabin in the country, outside of town."

Nate's eyes lit up. "I'm heading to Rockford myself."

"The evacuation collection point?" she asked.

He nodded. "An indoor soccer field they've turned into a shelter."

"If your family is there now, why didn't you go with them?"

The sigh that escaped his lips came out far more forcefully than he had intended. "Leave no man behind. Isn't that what the marines say?"

She stared back at him. "Sounds about right."

"My brother works at the power plant. I couldn't leave without at least trying to bring him with us."

"Why couldn't he get out on his own?" A look of confusion clouded Dakota's fine features.

"Probably because he's just as stubborn and loyal as I am. If there was a way to save the plant from melting down he wouldn't go until he'd tried it."

"And after?"

155

"Once it was too late, well, things quickly shifted from prevention to how to avoid the absolute worst-case scenario."

The girl's eyes narrowed slightly. "You were worried he would think you had abandoned him."

Nate rattled the fork in his now empty can of beans. "Maybe. But when I got there the guards played target practice with my truck. Once they were done trying to kill me, they said Evan had been taken to the hospital."

"Did they say which one?"

"No. Said they didn't know. And I can't entirely blame them. The whole situation was pure chaos. My guess is the ambulance would have headed for a hospital outside the exclusion zone. The Javon Bea Hospital is the biggest in Rockford. As good a place to start as any, I suppose." All this talk of hospitals and nuclear plants made him reach into his pocket and withdraw the Geiger counter.

"What's that?"

He switched it on and held out the wand. "It measures the amount of radiation in the air." The device clicked weakly.

"That's bad, isn't it?"

"It ain't good," he told her. "But it could be worse. The louder, more frantic the sound, the more radiation you're getting." He handed her a potassium iodide pill, then took one for himself.

"So we're safe in here?"

"Not safe. Less exposed."

"And out there?" she asked, pointing at the window and the blowing snow behind it.

Nate didn't reply to that one. The deep grooves of tension furrowing along his brow ridge were answer enough.

Chapter 27

No matter how you sliced it, there was no getting used to the sting on your cheeks when you first stepped out into the cold. Each time, it seemed to bite as painfully as it did the first.

Protected as best they could against the elements, Nate and Dakota made their way through the school's inner courtyard, past the remains of Lauren's pickup and out to the road.

Although she was at least a foot shorter than him, Dakota's ability to keep up was impressive. For both of them, the procedure remained the same. Search the white space before you for a dip in the snow, lift one foot, swing it forward, drop it down and hope something stopped its descent before you were up to your crotch. No one on earth could look cool trudging along in this fashion, but appearing foolish was a trade Nate was more than willing to make if it kept them alive.

Dakota pointed ahead to a strip where the wind had piled the snow up into a high ledge, leaving the space below it relatively shallow.

They made their way over, Nate already sweating his bits and pieces off. Dressing to face both the numbing cold as well as a bout of intense physical activity was an art he definitely had not yet mastered. By comparison, the girl appeared far more comfortable, in spite of the fact that her jacket was much thinner and lighter than his own.

Not five minutes in, they arrived at a decisive point. Either continue following the side roads back to Blackhawk Drive or cut through an open field and save some time.

The first meant they could keep an eye out for any robust vehicles able to make the journey and willing to take on two extra passengers—slim chance as that was. Off-roading on foot produced its own hazards. Namely, they would be traveling over virgin accumulation. The wind could very well have pushed some parts to over six feet in depth. Not to mention unforeseen barriers. Nate knew of at least one chest-high fence that ran along sections of Highway 2 between Byron and Rockford.

"If only we could find a snowplow," Dakota shouted in despair.

Nate tucked his head down, pulling at the end of a scarf to cover parts of his exposed face. All joking aside, her suggestion wasn't half bad, except it would mean heading back into town. Back toward the radiation they were trying so desperately to escape. Serious or not, her comment had jogged something loose in Nate's brain, a sight he remembered seeing a hundred times over the years as he'd driven between both towns.

159

"There's a farm just north of here," he indicated. "I suggest we head in that direction."

Dakota cinched her hood tight over the red beanie she was wearing. "What for? More food?"

"Transportation," he replied. There were horses there. He remembered seeing them from the highway this summer, grazing lazily in the sun, a sight so common in that old life it had faded into the low static of daily background noise.

"North it is," she agreed, aiming her gloved hand before them. "You do know how to ride a horse, don't you?"

"They don't call me Cowboy Nate for nothing." Nobody called him Cowboy Nate. But it was true. He had ridden a horse once or twice, nearly twenty years ago. He also knew there was no sense fretting over details before they got there. One of his favorite quotes by Mark Twain summed it up rather nicely. *Worrying is like paying a debt you don't owe.*

They turned off Blackhawk onto what, in warmer times, would have been a gravel country road. This was the dividing line between two radically different worlds, the urban and the rural. On one side, the top end of a mesh livestock fence poked just above the snowline. Beyond that stood a former pasture, now only a desolate field of blowing white powder. On the other side was a tree line broken only occasionally by the vague opening of a driveway. Since they had veered off, they had yet to see a single tire track. Could it be that the folks with nearby farms had opted to stay home and protect their property come what might? Had they ridden to Rockford themselves? Or had they already succumbed?

As they passed one property, Nate peered through the loose screen of trees, recognizing a red barn far in the distance. "This is it," he told her.

The lane was unbelievably long, and shaped like a giant question mark, winding around a clump of evergreens before finally arriving at the house. The structure itself was quaint. White, two-level with a wide wraparound porch and a stone chimney. He pointed. "No smoke."

Dakota nodded.

Approaching, they saw no sign of any vehicles. He conceded they could be buried beneath several feet of freshly fallen snow. Regardless, Nate was on his way to the front door when Dakota called him. "What are you doing?" she asked.

He looked at her, puzzled. "What do you mean what am I doing?"

"You said you wanted horses," she replied, her voice tinged with a hint of disbelief. She hooked a thumb over her shoulder. "Isn't the barn back that way?"

"It is, but I'm not a thief. Remember those friends of yours, the ones who threw you into that cage? I refuse to become one of them."

Dakota snickered. "I didn't mean steal, I meant borrow."

She was fighting him, at least on the outside. He could see that. She was part of a generation that had grown up downloading pirated copies of movies, books, music and software. What was stealing a few horses to someone not very well versed in the notion of property and ownership? Behind the snicker, however, Nate suspected Dakota knew he was right.

Nate climbed onto the porch and rapped at the door several times. Dakota stood back, staring out toward the road.

He was about to knock again when he followed her gaze and saw what she had been looking at. Fifty yards out stood the wolf. It was standing inside the tracks they'd made, eyeing them intently. The sight made Nate's pulse quicken.

"What do you think Shadow wants?" Dakota asked.

"Shadow? I thought you said he didn't belong to you?"

"You can't own a wild animal," she replied, her eyes never leaving the beast. "Not the way people own a poodle or a turtle. We were also cell mates, don't forget. Sure, it wasn't for more than a few hours, but we developed a kind of bond, I guess. I named him the minute I saw the dark patches of fur around his eyes."

Nate was looking into those feral eyes right now and not entirely sure what to think. Was the creature stalking them? Waiting for the weather to weaken them? Or was it hoping for something else?

Reluctantly, Nate turned his back for one final assault on the door. He decided to knock the way cops do when carrying out an arrest warrant.

Several minutes passed with still no result. Nate swung around to find Dakota, bobbing up and down, trying to stay warm. "All right, you win. Let's go check out the barn."

The more he thought of it, the simpler the argument in favor of liberating the horses became. Without a doubt, anything left behind in Byron was going to die— if not by starvation, then by the constant bombardment

162

of radiation in the atmosphere. Regardless of what people might have told themselves, once you left town, there was no coming back.

Nate scanned the snowline for the wolf. He was nowhere to be seen. It seemed Shadow was living up to the name Dakota had given him.

Once they reached the barn, Nate was relieved to see the door was a large side slider rather than the kind you opened by pulling outward, a task that would have wasted precious time and energy given the depth of the snow piled up against it.

Both Nate and Dakota leaned against the side of the structure and pushed with all their might, grunting from the effort. Slowly, the door began to move. Soon enough, they had created enough space for a tractor to come and go.

Upon entering, they were hit at once by the smell of hay mixed with the pungent odor of manure. Dakota plugged her nose with the end of her mitten. "Oh, that's strong."

Nate laughed. "It's not that bad. Besides, I'll gladly put up with a bit of stink if it gets us to Rockford in one piece."

He got no argument there. The only sound came from the stalls where three horses were whinnying. Two of them stuck their heads out, eyeing the newcomers with uncertainty. They were used to seeing the farmer, Nate assumed, not a couple of strangers wrapped from head to foot. Nate removed his beanie and gloves and approached a chestnut mare closest to them. He held out his hand, palm up. The horse's nimble lips searched for food, tickling him with her whiskers.

"Give him one of these," Dakota said, ripping open a bag of carrots on a nearby table and bringing him one.

"It's a she, not a he," Nate corrected her as he took the carrot, offered it to the mare. He grinned as she gobbled it down greedily. "Be careful your fingers don't get nipped. Hold your hand flat like this when you feed them."

Dakota approached a male Appaloosa, a popular breed created long ago by the Nez Perce Indian tribe. Like the mare, the Appaloosa eagerly took the carrot from Dakota's hand. She giggled with glee. She then fed the third horse, an aging draft animal that looked old and maybe a little grouchy.

"Watch that last one," Nate warned. "An angry horse is a dangerous horse, no matter how old they are."

But even Nate's caution couldn't wipe the enthusiasm from the young girl's face. "Oh, my God, his teeth look just like my grandma's. She used to grind them at night until they got real flat. Wow, I never knew humans could have horse teeth too."

Nate rolled back on his heels, laughing. The levity, however, was cut short by the sound of a shotgun being racked.

He spun, attempting to swing the AR around.

"Try it and it'll be the last thing you do," the man barked. He had both barrels trained on the center of Nate's chest.

Dakota was slowly reaching into her pocket where she kept the Glock she'd taken off Gabby. Nate signaled for her to stop.

"Same goes for you, missy," the man said.

Dakota raised her arms, scowling.

164

"Now, you wanna tell me what you're doing on my property?" His eyes were road-mapped with red lines. His skin was deathly pale.

"Are you feeling all right?" Nate asked, genuinely concerned. "You don't look so well."

"Never mind that," the farmer shouted. "I don't believe you broke in just to feed my horses."

"We tried knocking at the door," Nate replied in an attempt to explain.

"Yeah, we heard you pounding away. Sounded like you was trying to break in." The man coughed, removing one hand from his shotgun to instinctively cover his mouth. When he pulled it away, Nate saw blood there.

Nate shook his head. "This area isn't safe. There's been a meltdown at the plant, which is why we're trying to get out of town."

The farmer's face scrunched up. "The plant?"

"Yeah. Listen, when did you start feeling this way?" Nate asked.

"I'm perfectly fine," the man countered. "The lights been out a couple days. You get dumped on with this much snow, that sort of thing is bound to happen. 'Sides, I haven't heard nothing about any problems at the power plant."

"The whole town's been evacuated," Dakota said, the edges of her mouth drawn down in fear. "Anyone who stays behind is going to die."

"Harold," a woman's voice called from outside. "Is everything okay?"

"Gertie, you stay where you are. I've got the situation…" The farmer's words suddenly trailed off. His body was swaying like a tall reed in a brisk wind. One

165

stray hand reached out to stabilize him and failed to grasp anything useful. He let out a sigh and crumpled to his knees. Nate rushed to catch him.

"Oh, Harold," his wife said, stumbling in boots a few sizes too big for her. "What have you done to him?"

"Nothing, ma'am," Nate said, trying to keep the man upright. Harold's eyes were fluttering. "He fainted. We need to get him back inside."

Nate shouldered Harold's shotgun while Dakota moved in next to him and grabbed Harold's free elbow. Together, they got the old man on his feet and headed back to the house. Gertie walked ahead of them, turning around every few seconds, a terrified look on her pallid features. "Please don't hurt him," she kept saying.

Nate had no intention of doing anything of the sort, in spite of nearly getting shot for the second time in the past twenty-four hours.

With great effort, they reached the farmhouse. Gertie held open the door. "Set him on the couch while I make a fire," she told them.

The interior looked like something out of a Rockwell painting—old chairs and sofas next to round tables draped in lace dotted with family photos and antique lamps. If nothing else, the place was cozy.

They carefully deposited Harold onto the sofa, setting a pillow beneath his head. Nate wiped a thick layer of sweat from his own brow.

Dakota noticed this. "I'm sorry to be the one to tell you, but you're not dressed right for winter."

"What do you mean?"

"Your skin can't breathe," she told him. "I know a thing or two about dealing with cold weather and you're doing it all wrong."

Nate felt something stinging and he suspected it was his pride. "I'm wearing a t-shirt, sweater and winter jacket," he said, as if to prove his point.

"Exactly. You're dressed fine for someone going on a sleigh ride or something." That last part made her giggle. "Layering's the key. I'll bet every time you find yourself walking outside, a big old bucket of sweat goes rolling down your back."

Nate's eyes fell. "Not a bucket."

That also made her smile. "Okay, how about a pint glass then?"

"Fair enough."

"You start with breathable fabrics, like polyester. Long sleeves. Add another layer for warmth if needed. Then there's your jacket. It doesn't need to be heavy-duty. Light and windproof are far more important."

Nate smirked. "I thought I was the prepper here. How do you know all this stuff?"

Dakota batted her eyelashes. "A girl never tells."

Harold made a noise and it drew their attention.

"I told him not to go out there," Gertie said, sighing, as she brought the flame from a lighter to handfuls of crumpled paper in the fireplace. "Sometimes he can be as stubborn as a lop-eared mule."

Both Nate and Dakota cracked a smile at that.

"He's just like his son, I tell you," she went on, fanning the flames with the sports section. "Harold Junior. Goes by Harry. He's in real estate in Chicago. A real hotshot, too." Her voice suddenly took on the

167

mournful quality of a bereft mother. "He and Harold had words some time ago and we haven't heard from him since."

"I'm sorry to hear that," Nate said, meaning every word of it. He knew something about loss. "How long ago was that?" He was trying hard not to sound like he was interrogating a witness, a carryover from his days as a PI.

Gertie stopped fanning and starred up at the ceiling. "Oh, four, maybe five years. It's been a while."

"Didn't you say your mother worked in real estate in Chicago?" Nate asked Dakota on the off chance the two might have known each other.

The girl looked suddenly very uncomfortable. "Well, she did, a bit."

A deep line formed across Nate's forehead. "A bit? I thought you said she was one of the top agents in the city?"

Gertie perked up. "Then maybe she knew my son."

"I doubt it," Dakota said, sounding firm and maybe even a little dismissive. "Besides, I haven't a clue who she may or may not have known."

"What sort of real estate did she sell?" Gertie asked, turning just enough to lock eyes with the girl.

Dakota shrugged. "To be honest, I'm not sure. I said she was in real estate. All I know is that she sometimes showed people apartments."

There was a natural tendency in teenagers to inflate and exaggerate the exploits and wealth of their parents. That social pressure on young people might have always existed, but was particularly potent in today's day and age. With the internet, your competition wasn't only the kids on your block or at school. You were held up next to kids from around the world. It was hardly a surprise that under such circumstances the truth tended to get lost between layers of necessary fabrication, a survival tactic designed to ward off insignificance and loneliness.

Harold coughed, bringing only the slightest touch of color into his cheeks.

"Your husband's very sick," Nate said bluntly. The time for delicacy was long gone. He removed the Geiger from his pocket and switched it on. It crackled to life, stronger now than it had been at the school. "I believe he may have radiation poisoning."

She stopped. "Radiation? But from what?"

Nate explained the situation in as much detail as the circumstances would allow. "We don't mean you any harm. I hope you can see that now. We thought no one was home and were going to use your horses to get to Rockford."

"Our horses?" The flesh around Gertie's chin was loose and jiggled whenever she spoke.

"There's too much snow," Dakota explained. "I mean, look at your own cars, they're buried. You'd need a tank to make it through."

"That's assuming the highway itself isn't clogged with abandoned vehicles."

Gertie studied Dakota's face, then Nate's. "I'm sorry to be so rude, but you and your daughter look nothing alike."

Dakota blushed. "He's not my dad, just a…"

"Guy who was in the right place at the right time," Nate said, letting her off the hook.

Harold moaned, his eyes fluttering. "Let's get him some water," Nate suggested.

Gertie agreed and headed into the kitchen.

Dakota whispered to Nate, "Do you think this guy has a tractor?"

"He might. Why?"

"Well, wouldn't it make more sense to ride that thing to Rockford, rather than a pair of horses?"

Nate thought it over for a second, his eyes bright and contemplative. "It would have an easier time handling the snow. We'd also be just as exposed as we would on horseback. Then there's the highway. A single pileup could be enough to block us."

Dakota's mood soured with Nate's dire prediction.

Their options were few to begin with and seemed to be dwindling by the minute. Harold's eyes came open slowly and he pushed himself upright. "What are you doing in my house?" he bellowed.

"It's all right," Gertie said, returning with a glass of water. "You collapsed out in the barn. If they'd meant you harm, they would have simply left you there."

Harold grunted and gulped the water down in two mouthfuls.

The heat from the fireplace begged them to draw this moment out as long as they could. But the blood Harold had coughed up earlier had made it clear the longer they stayed, the sicker they would become.

"The gentleman here thinks you're suffering from radiation poisoning," Gertie told him.

Nate reached into his bag and produced three potassium iodide tablets. "Take one of these every

170

twenty-four hours. I know it isn't much, but at least it should counteract some of the effects."

"But why me and not you?" Harold asked, taking the pills and glaring down at them.

"Everyone's different," Dakota said, answering his question. "Age might play a factor. Along with genetics. It's hard to say, really. There are so many variables."

"And how do you know that?" Harold asked, skeptically.

"My intro to biology class," she replied. "It was the only class in school that I liked."

Harold let out a quiet snicker. "Never had much use for school and I don't think it had much use for me either. Got all my education working the land, growing corn and what not." His eyes glazed over for a moment, lost in a bout of nostalgia.

Gertie reached down and rubbed the side of her husband's stubbled face.

"We appreciate your hospitality," Nate told them. "But Dakota and I need to be getting on. Now that we know someone lives here, is there a way we can buy two of your horses?"

One of Harold's eyebrows perked up. "Suppose it depends on how much."

"You weren't watching the news before the lights went out, were you?" Nate asked.

"Gertie watches the television. Not me."

"It looks like the same people who cut the power also crashed our major financial institutions."

"So you're saying you have no money," Harold replied, pushing himself up on one elbow. "That takes 'the check's in the mail' to a whole new level." Gertie smiled too and Nate had no choice but to grin and bear it.

"Cash won't do you any good," Nate told them. Not least because the town was empty of people and cash registers wouldn't be operational for months, if ever.

"All right, give me your best offer then," Harold said, one hand pressed down into the sofa cushion as he propped himself into a seated position.

Nate grew quiet for a moment, searching through his bag. "How about three more potassium iodide pills, a can of beans and six double-aught buck shotgun shells?"

Harold's gaze moved to the AR Nate had rested against the seat next to him. "I like your rifle."

"I can't give you the AR, I'm afraid. But I can throw in my Remington 870 pump-action shotgun along with twelve shells of double-aught buck."

"Plus the pills and whatnot?" Harold's road-map eyes were gleaming.

"Sure, why not."

The old man held out a meaty paw. "Deal then." They shook. He turned to Dakota and did the same. "Pleasure doing business with you, young lady."

The smile on Dakota's face wavered and then fell. "Now I just need to figure out how to ride a horse."

Chapter 28

Thirty minutes later, Nate and Dakota were back in the barn, making some final preparations before they departed. Gertie came with them, if for no other reason than to be sure they got what was owed to them in the trade.

Both horses had a name, which surprised neither Nate or his young traveling companion. The chocolate-colored mare was called Sundae, as in a chocolate sundae, probably on account of her dark coat. The Appaloosian male with his camo-patterned design of white and brown hair was called Wayne, as in John Wayne. Like the actor, the horse was robust and brimming with quiet confidence. By comparison, Sundae was strong-willed and prone to whinny at the slightest provocation.

Once the saddles and bridle had been fitted, Gertie brought them each a set of leather saddle bags. "Won't have much use for these, not with the riding horses gone. You might as well fill them with carrots and what not. Sundae's got something of an appetite." The old woman smiled warmly. "Oh, and you should also take one of these each." She pointed to a bushel of hay. "With this weather, there won't be any grazing. The food you carry is all you're likely to get."

They thanked her, each taking turns giving her a hug. Nate wanted to bring both of them along, but he also knew that was far from realistic. Harold was far too sick to travel. Even more apparent was that Gertie would never leave his side. Their only salvation lay in the hope that this would all soon be over.

Nate then took a moment to go over the basics of western-style horseback riding. Now that this had gone from idea to a full-blown reality, Dakota's face had started filling with tension. Her lips were drawn into a thin line and her pupils were dilated. "For starters, use your heels to get her going and the reins to steer. If she starts going too fast, pull back on the reins, but not too hard. You'll be behind following. Chances are good Sundae here won't want to let Wayne out of her sight, so just let her do all the work."

Dakota nodded and swallowed.

"You're a brave young woman," Gertie said, rubbing her back. "I wish growing up I'd had a pinch of your gumption."

Nate helped her onto Sundae, before he mounted into his own saddle. Wayne backed up a few feet, blowing warm air through his lips until Nate used the reins to bring him to a stop. For her part, Sundae led Dakota over to a bale of hay and started eating.

"Don't forget who's boss," Nate reminded her.

Like an old pro, Dakota swung the reins to the left and nudged Sundae with the heels of her boots. The horse grunted and then complied.

Together, they headed out of the barn and back into the deep snow.

•••

In short order, they retraced their steps up the drive and back onto the road. The horses seemed to have a slightly easier time of it, especially in well-traversed areas. Although the real test, Nate knew, was yet to come.

Give or take, there were still four or five hours until the sun went down. With any luck, they would find somewhere along the highway to camp overnight and be in Rockford early the following morning. Their arrival would also mark more than reuniting with loved ones. It would mark their departure from the exclusion zone and the radiation that was already busy claiming Harold's life and probably his wife's too.

Within thirty minutes, Dakota was comfortable enough to break the follow-the-leader routine and bring her horse alongside his.

"Wayne's got bad gas," she said, waving her hand in front of her nose. "Wind's blowing it right in my face. Sundae may not mind, but I was about to puke."

Nate let out a resounding belly laugh. "Maybe he's allergic to carrots. I'll keep that in mind at snack time."

They reached Blackhawk and turned left. Eventually this road would become Highway 2. Along the way, a handful of mounds marked the location of abandoned vehicles, buried in the snow along with whoever had opted to stay huddled inside. He couldn't help recalling Jessie, the woman he'd met yesterday, hiding in her car, waiting for someone who would probably never show. The more time passed, the more certain he was becoming that just such a scene was playing out all over the country.

While to the north the enemy might be the cold and the snow, further south, the heat was an adversary no less deadly. Technology was what we used to ease our discomfort. Too cold? Crank the heat. Too hot? Throw on some AC. He swallowed hard, thinking of Amy. Funny how even the most random trains of thought had a habit of leading back to her. By this time tomorrow, she would be back in his arms. Nate didn't simply want to believe that. He needed to. Anything to keep pushing back against that freezing arctic wind.

Speaking of which, since changing direction, the blowing snow was now coming from right to left, numbing that side of his body. He winced, not from the cold this time. The constant act of arching his legs around Wayne's generous torso was pushing against his knee. Three operations later and the thing was no less defective. That was something they didn't tell you growing up—that your parts wore out and needed replacing. Made him feel like an old jalopy sometimes, a Model T in a world of Teslas. Maybe Dakota's colorful description of him hadn't been that far off after all.

Up ahead, the road curved gently to the right, hugging the frozen Rock River. On the other was one farmer's field after another, fenced off and stretching to a range of nearby hills. It would be this way for much of the journey to Rockford. More importantly, any sign of tire tracks had long since faded. Whoever intended on fleeing Byron had already done so. At least, that was how it seemed.

Dakota was riding next to him, moving in the saddle as Sundae worked her way across the challenging terrain. Just past her, something in the field caught his attention—a dark figure, working its way through the deep powder. This guy wasn't giving up.

Nate pointed and Dakota turned her head to see.

"Shadow," she said, sounding pleasantly surprised. "I had a feeling we'd see him again."

The feeling brewing inside Nate was far from pleasant or surprised, however. This was a wild animal, one that had been following them since they left the middle school. He recognized that it could have attacked them then and it hadn't. That had to mean something. But can you ever really trust a wild creature?

"He isn't a poodle or a stuffed animal," Nate reminded her.

She spun and scrunched up her face. "Uh, duh."

"Did you know that every year dozens of people around the world are killed at zoos climbing into polar bear enclosures or lion cages? The ones that survive, you know what they say?"

"'I wanted to pet Simba?'"

"Exactly. They just got done watching *Lion King* for the hundredth time and wanted to get his autograph."

She laughed. "No way."

"I'm serious," he replied, his gaze periodically moving past her. Shadow was still visible, navigating the weather with impressive ease. "You can't make this stuff up." Nate wasn't out to denigrate such a majestic creature. Nevertheless, he hoped Shadow wouldn't do something stupid and force his hand.

He decided to change the subject. "I noticed you got a bit funny back there at the farm when your mom's job came up."

Dakota's gaze was focused down the road, her face an impenetrable mask.

"I understand you didn't get along with your folks, but I'm sure, given all that's happened, they deserve to know you're all right."

"It's complicated," she said in return, an unstable ice shelf of emotion building behind her normally soft voice. "Frankly, I don't think they give a damn whether I'm alive or dead."

"All I know is if you were my daughter and you were taken, I'd be heartbroken. I can't imagine they'd be any different." Although he said the words to Dakota, he might as well have been talking to his long-lost sister, Marie.

The girl looked at him, her eyes gleaming. "You would come find me, wouldn't you?"

"Sure I would." Nate quickly realized he had probably said the wrong thing because Dakota bent forward, her body convulsing. With one hand on the pommel of his saddle, he leaned over and rubbed her back. "I'm sure they love you, even if they don't have a clue how to show it."

"It's not that," she said, the tears still in her throat. "The stuff about my parents…"

"What about it?"

Dakota's eyes were sullen and downcast. "I lied."

Chapter 29

Nate stared at the girl, not entirely sure what to think. "Then I take it your father isn't an entrepreneur and your mother isn't in real estate."

Dakota fidgeted with the reins, refusing to look at him. "The only way my dad could be counted as a businessman was hawking the pain pills my parents didn't take themselves. They weren't successful or brilliant. You couldn't even say they were ordinary. Subpar. Losers. Take your pick. One is as good as another. When they weren't whacked out of their minds on drugs, they were usually fighting. Throwing things. Hitting each other with whatever was around. Ashtrays, cans of Coke, you name it. A real battle royale, just like the videogame. You know, the one all the kids are playing."

Yeah, Nate knew a thing or two about that. "You were ashamed. I get that. Although I don't like that you lied to me."

"I don't know why I did it. At the time, I guess it somehow felt like the right thing to do. I didn't want you to hate me."

"Hate you for having lousy parents? Do I look like that big a prick?"

The hint of a smile. "You did look a little frightening when I first met you," she admitted. "I wasn't sure if you were freeing me or whether I was simply changing captors."

Nate's eyes returned to the road. "You're free to go whenever you'd like."

She looked down again. "I know. I'm thankful. It's partly why I thought you deserved to hear the truth."

"Sooner or later, I would have figured it out on my own," he said before tapping the side of his nose. "Call it a cop's instinct, but I could tell back at the farmhouse something wasn't adding up."

"I know. I wanted you to hear it from me, rather than finding out some other way."

The horses struggled to blink away the fat blowing flakes coming at them. Ahead lay a sea of white, broken only by a screen of trees to their right, a mix of old elm and evergreens. There was no sign of any cars or trucks anymore, except those buried under several inches and in some cases feet of snow. Nate's thoughts circled back to the fib Dakota had told him. "And your folks. Your real folks. Where are they now?"

She shrugged. "No idea. Dead for all I know. The state eventually came and took me away. Sent me to live with my uncle Roger, the only known relative we had. He had a house in Rockford. He was older than you by at least ten years and never had kids. It was a big

180

adjustment for the both of us, is probably the nice way of saying it. Though I will say he taught me a lot in the short few months we lived together. He was one of those survivalist types."

"What happened?"

Dakota made the international sign of a bottle with her thumb and pinky and tilted it at her lips.

"Oh," Nate said, getting the implication. "Addiction runs in your family."

"It's why I try to never touch the stuff, even if I'm not allowed to do so legally. When he was sober, Uncle Roger would bring me fishing and hunting. Taught me how to survive in the wilderness and make my way around if I ever became lost. Learned more in my short time with him than I did in all my years of formal schooling."

"I don't doubt that one bit. The education system needs to be seriously reformed."

Dakota couldn't disagree more. "Reformed? I think the whole damn system needs to be torn down and remade, the way some people gut the inside of their house and rebuild it from the ground up."

Nate's eyebrows did a little dance. "Looks like you may have gotten your wish."

A light flashed behind Dakota's eyes. "That's what Uncle Roger always hoped for. He had a room at the back of his house and sometimes I'd hear him in there talking. He had one of those old-school radio thingies. You know, the ones with the wires and the mic."

"A shortwave?" Nate asked, turning in the saddle, his eyes intense and staring right at her.

"Yeah, that's the one."

"What was his call sign?"

"Call sign?"

"His nickname over the radio. His moniker."

"Oh, I thought it was Ranger, but I was wrong. He called himself Renegade."

Nate snorted with a burst of laughter.

"Why are you laughing? I'm telling the truth," Dakota said, sounding defensive.

"I know you are. I spoke to your uncle the day after the lights went out. He left me with the impression that he was very knowledgeable."

"He is. You know, he wasn't a mean drunk at all. I guess the booze meant he wasn't very..." She looked up, scanning for the right word.

"Resilient?" Nate inquired.

"No, dependable. I was sent to foster homes not long after. Try being bounced between every small town in a fifty-mile radius. Landed in one house where the husband liked to let his hands wander, if you know what I mean. Tried to put his thumb in my mouth and I bit down hard enough to hear the bone crunch. Another family would send me around to babysit and steal the money I earned. And if I tried to fight back, they'd keep me locked in my room without food or water for hours. The last family I was with, they weren't cruel, not in the same way. All they wanted was the government check. And when the lights went out, they skipped out faster than green grass through a goose."

Nate's eyes widened. "They left you behind?"

Dakota nodded, the corner of her mouth turned down in an 'are you really all that surprised?' kinda look.

"I woke up to find myself alone. On the kitchen counter was a note telling me to get myself to Rockford."

"Wow, that's cold."

"If the government was done paying, they were done caring, I suppose. They had a crap car for winter. I'd hear the man—Greg was his name—complaining about not having enough to buy a new one. A Nissan hatchback or maybe it was a Honda." She pointed at a passing snow mound. "Anyway. Wouldn't surprise me if it was them under one of these frozen heaps."

An image of the dead boy sticking out of the snow drift flashed before Nate's eyes. In normal times, the melting snows in springtime might only reveal a mountain of dog turds. But he had a sinking feeling the next spring something far more ghastly than turds would litter the streets and sidewalks.

"I had been up for a grand total of three minutes," Dakota went on, using her hand to block a sudden gust of cold wind, "still trying to figure out whether or not I was being pranked, when I heard the door open. Only it wasn't my foster parents come back to get me. It was my foster mother's lowlife brother, Marvin."

"Marvin," Nate repeated, his expression a mask of distaste.

"Came in with three of his lowlife friends and grabbed me along with a few of my things and threw me in a cage. Then you showed up and put two in his chest."

Sudden understanding flashed on Nate's face. Marvin was the guy he had nicknamed Ugly. "Did you ever find out what they'd intended to do with you?" he asked, not entirely sure he wanted to hear the answer.

183

Mercifully, Dakota shook her head. "I heard them talking about a guy they worked for. Someone named Jakes. Left me with the distinct impression they were going to try to sell me."

"That won't happen," Nate assured her. "Not as long as I'm around." He would have liked to have said she believed him. But he also understood getting bounced around from one foster home to another had a habit of eroding a person's faith in their fellow man much the way water could eat into a cliffside. Once gone, it was darn well impossible to get it back.

"I hope we never need to test that promise," she said, thoughtfully.

"It took guts to come clean," Nate told her. "That's quite a life you've had. I don't blame you for not wanting to share the full truth." He tried to grin, but his frozen lips refused to budge. "Looking down the barrel at my fortieth, it shouldn't come as a surprise that I've done a few things I'm not terribly proud of. Most of it's just stuff a person has to deal and get on with. That's life, right? But there's one that I can't shake. Something big I can't help feeling responsible for."

"Please tell me you didn't pull the wrong switch and shut the power off by mistake." She looked annoyed and that made Nate laugh.

"No, hackers did that. No doubt very skillful ones too. What I'm getting at is that I feel responsible for the meltdown."

"Responsible how? Do you work there?"

"I did for a number of years. I was in charge of cyber-security. It was my job to spot potential vulnerabilities and plug those holes before the bad guys could exploit them. When I discovered that the Byron plant's anti-hacking protocols were lacking, I tried to address it, but the company wouldn't let me."

"How on earth is that your fault?"

"The weight might not rest entirely on my shoulders, but I can feel it pressing down nonetheless. It happens whenever I see a dead body. It happened at the farmhouse too when Harold started coughing up blood. I could have done more. Gone to the local news station maybe. I don't know. Somehow, I should have forced the company's hand, even if doing so would have meant getting sued into oblivion."

"You're talking about a suicide mission," Dakota said, compassion filling her young face. "Guys like that can sue you for everything you're worth. Leave you and your family penniless. If your only choice is a kamikaze mission, that's not really a choice. You see what I mean? All of that blood is on the hands of the people who refused to listen. I say that as I sit here on Sundae's hard, incredibly uncomfortable saddle, freezing my butt off. You did everything any reasonable person could be expected to do. You're not the bad guy in all this. The jerks who hacked in and shut everything down, they're the ones who will need to answer for what they've done."

"I suppose you're right," he told her, feeling a little more convinced. "It's our job to survive long enough to rebuild what we once knew."

Dakota held the pommel with both hands and straightened her back. "Or maybe something better."

Chapter 30

They were a little better than halfway to Rockford when the light began to fade.

"We'll need to stay out overnight," Nate told her. "Give the horses a chance to recover and hopefully catch some shut-eye ourselves."

Dakota scanned their surroundings. "You have something in mind?"

"Well, I figured we could dig out one of these cars and use them as shelter. Assuming, of course, it's empty." His comment had a gallows quality he hadn't intended.

"What about Sundae and Wayne? We can't just leave them on the road."

Nate pointed to the deep snow. "They won't get hit by a car, if that's what you're worried about. Nothing short of a main battle tank could make it through a dumping this heavy."

"I think I have a better idea," she said, her gaze wandering to the forest that stretched along this part of the highway.

After considering it for a moment, he quickly concluded that if her idea proved to be a waste of time, they could always come back and camp out in one of the abandoned vehicles.

They veered off the path, leading the horses up a small incline and into a cluster of trees. The snow here was untouched and much deeper. The horses grunted as they struggled to place one hoof in front of the other. Fifteen yards in, they reached a small clearing. Dakota pulled Sundae to a stop. "This is where we'll build it," she said enigmatically.

"Build what?" Nate wondered, more confused at this point than worried.

"A snow hut," she told him nonchalantly. "Uh, Natives call them quinzhees."

Ah, yes. Nate remembered reading something about them once on a survivalist website, but in all his years of prepping, he had never actually bothered to make one.

"Couple years ago, Uncle Roger and I made one on a winter hunting trip in the Adirondacks. Takes a while to get started, but you'll see it's well worth it in the end."

After dismounting, they tied the horses to a nearby tree and marked out a circular section in the snow about twenty feet in diameter. Afterward, they began piling snow into the center. Nate went into his go-bag and produced a small tactical survival shovel he'd purchased online. The compact size made the work feel even more backbreaking than it was, but it certainly increased the speed. Within the span of an hour, they had created a pile eight feet tall.

187

After they were done, Nate and Dakota stood, admiring their handiwork.

"Now we let it sit for at least two hours."

She was right. It would take time for the snow particles to rebind into an ultra-hard dome. But once the two hours had passed, Nate and his spade would get to work once more, carving out the inside in order to create a living space.

Dakota's arms were folded over her chest. "If we make the entrance right, it should block the wind and provide a really comfortable shelter."

"In the meantime," Nate said, "I'll gather some wood for a fire."

Less than twenty feet away, a fallen birch tree sat at a forty-five-degree angle, a fortuitous discovery since birch made great firewood. Likewise, the paper-like quality of the tree's bark made for terrific kindling. For this task, he employed a small hatchet, another online purchase. After scanning the area around him for threats—the wolf was still around here somewhere—and finding none, Nate got to work, collecting what he could.

Meanwhile, back at camp, Dakota was busy clearing out a section for the firepit. Once she was done, she layered it with evergreen branches. This would keep the wood dry and also make it easier to light. She then collected another, larger bundle and set it aside for later use inside the snow hut.

The insulating quality of the forest reduced the gale from the highway to a cool, gentle breeze. Nate marveled at how quiet it was here, maybe even serene, a sense tainted whenever the sharp end of his hatchet dug into the birch tree. Already he had set aside a generous portion of kindling and was working on adding a few larger pieces. He had camped out in summer long enough to know how much wood a fire could consume in a single session. Taking a moment to glance over at Dakota's firepit, he appreciated how she had dug down into the snow to create a sitting area. This would not only reduce visibility to any passersby on the highway, digging the hole would also prevent the campfire from collapsing as the snow melted from the heat.

Returning his attention to the fallen tree, Nate raised the hatchet and brought it down into the groove he'd recently created. It should have been the coup de grâce. Except, instead of hearing a satisfying thunk, all he got was a discordant clang, followed by a plop. He stared down in disbelief at the bladeless hatchet handle. The metal end had fallen off, landing at his feet in a clump of deep snow.

He heard giggling from the camp site and a muffled sound as Dakota clapped her gloved mittens together. "Bravo!"

He held up the handle and waved it around proudly. "Would you believe I paid a hundred bucks for this thing? Twelve hundred reviews on Amazon with four point seven stars out of five."

Dakota laughed even harder, her cheeks flushing a deeper shade of pink.

He returned to the dead tree and brought the bottom of his fist down on the splintered end. It snapped off at once and fell into his pile. Afterward, he fished the hatchet blade out of the snow and reattached it.

With camp ready and the horses fed, they set about lighting the fire. Both he and Dakota rummaged in their respective bags for the necessary gear. Seconds later, Nate emerged with a flint fire starter. The device was divided into two parts. The first consisted of a three-inch rod of magnesium and flint. Next to that was the striker. The process was simple enough. You began by shaving off magnesium and setting it on a uniform surface. Then you ran the striker along the flint, directing the sparks at the shavings. Once the shavings caught, you could then begin adding your kindling, going from the smallest pieces on up. Given that humans had discovered the art of making fire tens, if not hundreds of thousands of years ago, you could hand the kit to a young child and they'd have the details figured out in no time.

"Or we could use this," Dakota said, flashing the lighter she had just removed from her bag.

Nate waved his hand. "Okay, smartypants. Be my guest."

She lit the birch bark with the lighter and the flames began to spread at once, the wood positioned above it crackling and popping. The waves of heat dancing along his frozen cheeks felt amazing.

"I needed a knife earlier to cut the evergreen branches," Dakota began.

"There was one in my bag," he told her.

She held it up. "Yeah, I found it. Hope you don't mind. You were so concentrated on showing that fallen tree who's boss, I felt bad disturbing you."

"That's fine. My go-bag doesn't contain any secrets."

Dakota nodded. "Yeah, I noticed. It also doesn't contain anything all that useful."

Nate straightened. "What do you mean?"

She was trying hard to hide the smile on her face. "I'm just saying you've got a lot of gadgets that look great but aren't all they're chalked up to be."

"You mean the hatchet?" It was back in one piece and he held it up as if to prove the point.

"Yes, but more than that. For instance, there's the tactical flashlight that's supposed to be waterproof, but isn't. A compass that doesn't work. The knife that has the name of that survival guy on TV. In and of itself, a celebrity-endorsed product might not be the end of the world, but after cutting a few saplings, I can already see the blade is starting to dull."

Nate threw his head back and bellowed laughter. "Okay, enough. I get your point."

"If there was one thing my uncle Roger taught me, it's that most of the kits sold online are junk made in China. In the nine months we spent together, I don't ever remember seeing him with any shiny, high-tech gear. He was a big believer in the KISS philosophy."

"Keep it simple, stupid," Nate said, agreeing. She was a smart little bugger, or at the very least observant. "It's funny. You collect all this stuff hoping you're never going to need to use it. But it makes you feel good. Makes you feel safe, like you're ready for the worst possible scenario. The truth is I'm starting to think that none of us are ever truly ready for a disaster of this magnitude." I learned my lesson the hard way with the hatchet." He plucked up the tactical spade. "Let's hope this holds out until after we finish the quinzhees."

After placing a fresh log on the fire, they tested the hardness of the shelter. Nate clambered up the side and stood on the dome, marveling at the structure's ability to carry his entire weight. Satisfied, they began to dig their way inside, Nate with the spade, Dakota behind him pulling out the icy snow and tossing it aside. Once a sizable sleeping space had been carved out, Dakota went in with the evergreen saplings she had cut down and made a decently insulated sleeping platform. It might not be the Ritz Carlton, but compared with the prospect of sleeping outside, it didn't feel far off.

The sun was gone by the time they were done. Thankfully, Dakota had tended to the fire so that by now there was a solid bed of coals. Now just about anything they tossed in would burn nicely.

Some time later, they were sitting in the warm glow, quietly eating a dinner of canned tuna and green beans, when the silence was broken by the sound of howling. Nearby, the horses began to whinny and stomp their hooves into the snow.

Nate perked up, his fork still in the act of stabbing at a stray bean. It was impossible to tell the distance between them and the beast. Dakota scanned the frozen river beside the highway.

"You see anything?" he asked, setting down the can and picking up his AR.

She shook her head, looking almost disappointed. "I'm waiting to hear if there's any kind of answer."

Then came the sound of movement through the trees. Nate sprang to his feet, aiming his rifle at the sound. "Draw your weapon," he ordered Dakota. Reaching into her coat pocket, she withdrew the Glock she'd taken from the thug who'd imprisoned her.

Whoever this was, they were getting closer, their movements slow and lumbering. If it was Shadow, he had one hell of a way of making an entrance.

"Don't shoot," a female voice called out from the darkness.

Nate hesitated and Dakota tensed. It seemed she was more wary of people than she was of wild, predatory animals.

The slender form of a woman stepped into the light. Her tight-fitting cream-colored jacket was dirty and she had a scarf wrapped around her face.

"Who are you?" Nate asked.

"My name's Brie," she replied. Her voice had a slightly raspy quality to it.

"All right, Brie, you mind uncovering your face?" Nate told her, in that deep authoritative voice he saved for situations such as this.

The woman unwrapped the scarf. She was attractive, with strands of blonde hair poking out from beneath her beanie. "We're friendly," she said. "I swear."

"We?" Dakota asked, a touch of alarm in her voice.

"I'm here with my husband Ed and my brother-in-law Dylan. We were heading to Byron when we saw the glow from your fire against the trees. Do you think we could warm up for a minute before we carry on? We could pay you."

Nate's expression remained impassive. "Let me get a look at your husband and your brother-in-law first."

Two men came forward into the light and removed their hats.

"This is Ed," the woman said, pointing to the man on her right. He was above average height, with striking eyes and nice features. The winter hat he was wearing had messed up his hair, revealing the beginnings of a receding hairline. Dylan was the other man, shorter than his brother by maybe six inches with a fuller head of hair, but with much bigger ears. The two men nodded.

193

"You can put the guns down," Ed said, in a soft, non-threatening voice. "We mean you folks no harm."

"I'll be the judge of that," Nate assured them. "Are you armed?"

Dylan shook his head. "Between the three of us we got a Remington hunting rifle and a half-dozen bullets."

Bullets were what fired through the barrel of a weapon. Cartridges were the entire assembly, which suggested to Nate that these people didn't really know what they were doing.

"Then I'll ask you to kindly unload the weapon and lean it against one of those trees," Nate instructed them.

"No problem, mister," Dylan said, swinging it off his shoulder and doing as he was asked.

Nate's rifle was still in the low ready position. "Just so we're all clear, if I find out any of you lied about being armed, I reserve the right to start shooting."

"Hey, we just wanna get warm," Brie said, frightened.

"Believe me, I'm not trying to be *that* guy," Nate told them. "I'm sure if the tables were turned you'd do the same."

Dylan returned from setting down the rifle. "We probably would."

Nate threw another log on the fire. Sparks flew up as the others gathered around, warming their hands by the flames. Dakota shuffled closer to where Nate was sitting, her Glock resting on her lap.

"Did I hear you right when you said you were heading to Byron?" Nate asked, his pulse beginning to settle. "You do know about the meltdown, right? If I were you, I'd avoid Byron like the plague."

194

"Yes, sir, we were warned," Ed told him, rubbing the tips of his fingers together. "Truth is, we're heading to check on my folks. I got a sneaking suspicion they didn't evacuate along with everyone else."

That got Nate's attention. "Did you come from Rockford?"

Brie nodded. "Yup. Left a good five hours ago. Hiking through this mess has been the toughest thing I've ever done."

"Tough is the understatement of the century," Ed spat. "Closer to a nightmare if you ask me."

"Where in Byron do your folks live?" Nate asked, thinking of the farming couple they had met and how many others might have also stayed behind.

"Canyon Street, I believe," Dylan replied.

Dakota stared into the flames of the fire, mesmerized.

"Over by the Safeway?"

Dylan nodded. "Yeah, that's right."

Nate watched as the brother-in-law removed the backpack he was wearing and began to unzip it. "Easy now," Nate said, a bolt of electricity running through his nervous system.

Dylan grinned widely. "I'm just getting a drink, man. Something to warm us up." Slowly, he reached in and came out with a bottle of Grey Goose vodka. "Nothing, but the finest for our new friends." He removed the cap with his teeth and then took a swig, offering some to Nate, who turned it down, then to Dakota. The girl looked over at Nate, who shook his head, indicating it wasn't a good idea.

She seemed to go back and forth in an invisible tug-of-war before saying, "One little sip can't hurt." She took the bottle and tilted it back, then wiped her lips with the back of her hand. "Whoa, that's strong." She offered it to Nate, who again refused.

"Come on, man," Dylan said. "It'll help you stay warm."

With strangers in their camp and a wolf on the loose, there was no way in hell he was gonna start knocking back shots of the hard stuff. "Thanks, but I'm gonna pass."

"Your loss," Dylan lamented, passing the vodka over to his brother, Ed.

The bottle made the rounds a few more times before Ed pointed with his finger. "What's that scratched into the side of your handgun?"

He was talking to Dakota. She glanced down at the Glock in her lap, seeming to notice the strange marking for the first time herself. It looked like a trident, etched into the slide with the tip of a sharp blade. "No clue," she said, truthfully. "I took it off some thug bastard who put me in a cage."

Brie was in mid-sip when she spat vodka into her lap. "A cage? What? Are you serious?"

Dakota nodded, her eyes a touch glassy and unfocused. She held up three fingers. "Not a word of a lie. Even locked me up next to a wolf."

Dylan burst into a wild cackle of laughter. "Should have stayed put. They might have sold you to the circus. Those French guys. You know, Serk due Soley."

The others bellowed laughter, their voices starting to carry. The sound was making them vulnerable. And as far as Nate was concerned, these travelers had more than worn out their welcome.

"What do you say we wrap this up?" he suggested. "The girl and I have a long day ahead of us tomorrow."

"Oh, come on, Nate, not yet," Dakota protested, reaching for the bottle. "I'm having fun."

In spite of the cold, Nate felt the blood rush into his cheeks. "First of all, you're too young to be drinking."

"Chill out, ma—" Dylan began before Nate cut him off.

"We're done," he insisted, his voice low and menacing.

The message was clear: *Keep on pushing, and I won't be held responsible for what happens next.*

"Okay, dude, no problem. We'll leave," Brie said, standing and straightening out her ski pants. "Before we leave, I gotta go to the bathroom." And with that she staggered off into the woods. Nate's eyes traced her movements as she disappeared into shadow. She had not headed toward the rifle Dylan had leaned up against the tree, but that paranoid part of his brain wondered nevertheless whether she intended on circling back to grab it.

Across from Nate, Ed and Dylan sat staring back at him.

"So where are you really headed?" Nate asked.

One of Ed's eyebrows perked up. "Excuse me?"

The expression on Nate's rugged face was cold, emotionless. "You heard me."

"What's the problem?" Dakota said. "These guys are our friends."

197

"Stay out of this," he barked, his stare solid, unwavering. He turned back to the two men. "You lied to us before and I was willing to let it go, but something tells me you're up to no good."

The AR was sitting next to Nate, close enough that he could grab hold and bring it to bear before either man could close the distance between them.

"I don't know what you're talking about," Dylan said, waving his hands before him.

"Byron has neither a Canyon Street nor a Safeway."

A dead cold silence followed for several seconds.

"We made a mistake, is all," Ed said. "Got confused." He pointed to the bottle of Grey Goose. "The booze. It's the booze that got us all turned around."

"You said it before you started drinking," Nate shot back. "Unless you want me to believe you're heading into an irradiated area, through deep snow, hydrating yourselves with shots of vodka."

They fell silent again.

"I'll ask you one last time, where were you headed?"

The fun-loving, easy-going glint faded from Dylan's eyes. "We found what we came looking for. Wasn't hard either. Tracks in the snow led us to the farm and then along the highway. It was almost as though you wanted to get caught."

Dakota let out an audible gasp right as the crack from a rifle shattered the cool night air. For Nate, everything after that seemed to slow to a crawl. The rifle round zipped past Nate's ear, thudding somewhere behind him. The same place where the horses were tied.

The animals erupted into a deafening racket of whinnies and cries.

Nate spotted the shooter outside of camp, little more than a silhouette. He stood, raising the AR, and managed to pop off two rounds before Dylan sprang to his feet and grabbed the rifle barrel, jerking it up and off target. Now all three men were standing, Ed and Dylan reaching into their respective jackets for what Nate could only assume were weapons. With the end of his AR still tightly held in Dylan's grip, his only chance was to draw his own. Next to him, Dakota sat frozen, her face locked in an expression of pure terror.

Nate's pistol was in a hip holster under his jacket. He reached for it, only vaguely aware of another, sleeker form rushing toward them from out of the darkness. A moment later, a mass of fur and teeth leapt into the ring of firelight, its mouth open and aiming for the soft part of Ed's neck. Ed was still fumbling for the gun in his jacket when the wolf's jaws clamped down with terrifying and lethal force, crushing his windpipe. Both forms collapsed onto the ground, the packed snow around them turning crimson as Shadow shook his head. Dylan stared down in utter horror, which gave Nate the brief opportunity he needed to raise his pistol and put a bullet behind the man's left temple. Dylan dropped next to his brother, both of them dead.

Nate then rushed to the edge of camp, ready to engage the shooter. Instead, he found Brie dead, the rifle lying next to her. It appeared the woman had done exactly what he hoped she wouldn't do.

Satisfied they were no longer in immediate danger, Nate collected the rifle and returned to camp. There he witnessed a sight he hadn't expected. Dakota was crouched next to the wolf, rubbing his chin.

"I'm not sure that's such a good idea," Nate said, eyeing them warily.

"What do you mean? He just helped us."

She did have a point. Nate reached out to show the beast some small sign of appreciation. His approach was met with a low growl from the back of Shadow's throat.

Nate retracted his hand, frowning. "He doesn't like me." He went into his bag anyway and grabbed a can of tuna. "Love or hate, I'm sure he's hungry." He opened it, took some in his hand and held it out. "Let's see what you do with this, big boy."

Shadow swung his large powerful neck around, the corners of his nose dancing at the smell of food.

"There you go," Nate said, triumphantly as the beast inched closer. "You don't hate old Nate as much as you thought, do you?"

Shadow looked up at him with those dark eyes surrounded in amber. The animal tilted his head and then backed up.

Dakota laughed. "Here, hand it over."

He did so. Dakota held the tuna in her open palm and at once Shadow went to town, licking her fingers even after it was all gone.

"Good doggie," the girl said, ruffling the fur on his head. She turned to Nate. "Don't worry. He'll warm up to you sooner or later." Then before Nate could reply, she said. "Listen, I wanted to apologize for before. I don't know what came over me."

"You have trouble with authority figures," Nate said, closing his go-bag. "I suppose I can't blame you, given your history and what not." He was referring to the time she'd spent being unceremoniously shuffled from one bad foster home to another. "Anyone else would feel the same way."

She quit scratching Shadow's chin. The wolf sat there, staring back at her with a look that said, *Hey, why'd you stop?* When it was clear the chin scratch was officially over, Shadow got up and sauntered off back into the woods.

Dakota watched him go. Her gaze then fell on the two dead men lying around the dying campfire. She held out her hands, wielding an imaginary gun. "I should have listened to you, I know that. But that's not why I'm ashamed, least not the only reason. When the shooting started, it felt like every joint in my body locked up. I was like the Tin Man in *The Wizard of Oz*. Beth, my very first foster mother, she played the movie all the time. Thought it would keep me occupied. She didn't realize I was way too old. Even so, it still left me yearning to click my heels and go back home. Not to my parents—they stopped representing home a long time ago—but to Uncle Roger. Of anyone, he'd be the most disappointed since I had a gun in my hand and I was too scared to use it."

Nate didn't say a word. He simply laid a hand on her shoulder. This young girl might have learned a trick or two about staying alive in the middle of winter, but she still had a lot to learn about overcoming the paralyzing effects of fear. Nate's years as a beat cop and more recently as a PI had helped to hone those particular skills.

"You also knew they were lying," she said, amazed.

"An old police trick," he explained. "You throw out false information during an interrogation and see if the suspect goes along. He mentioned Canyon Street and my antenna perked up at once. Not enough to start shooting, but enough to lay a trap. There isn't a Safeway grocery store anywhere in the county, so when he agreed his parents lived near one, I was convinced they were being deceitful." Nate glanced down at the two dead men. "We better drag these guys off and bury them under a few feet of snow. Let spring take care of the rest."

Dakota stood, glanced over her shoulder and let out a little cry. Nate swung around, still reaching for his pistol when he saw what she was looking at. His heart sank. One of the horses—Sundae—was lying in the snow, dead. The rifle shot meant for his head must have hit the mare instead.

"You bastards!" Dakota screamed, spinning around and firing two shots from her Glock into each of the dead men's bodies.

"Easy, girl," Nate said, pushing the pistol down and pulling her into a hug. "They already got what they deserved. Let's save the ammo. We're likely to cross paths with many others just as deserving."

Dakota glared down at the pistol in her hand, grimacing. "One of them said something right before you shot them. Do you remember?"

Nate did. "Yeah, that they'd been tracking us. I heard it, but I wasn't sure if he meant it literally or to mess with our heads."

She knelt down and collected one of the men's pistols from the snowpack and held it up to the firelight. She spun the weapon around to show Nate, creases of fear forming at the corners of her hazel eyes. Scratched into the slide was the same symbol as the Glock Dakota had taken from the thug in Byron. "What do you make of it?" she asked.

Nate studied it long and hard before answering. "Hard to say, but whatever it means, it can't be good."

Chapter 31

Day 5

Nate awoke early the next morning to soft whispers of light streaming in through the snow hut's narrow entrance. It had taken him a few hours before he felt comfortable enough to drift off. Dakota had faded almost at once, her nighttime breathing settling into the faintest hint of a snore. Had it been any louder, Nate would have recorded it, if for no other reason than to show her he wasn't the only one who could saw some zees.

He lay there for a while, zipped up in his compact winter sleeping bag, slowly digesting everything that had happened over the past few days. Recent as his memories were, many of his experiences since the blackout had somehow taken on the consistency of a fine mist. The more you tried to close your hand around it, the quicker it evaded your grasp. The sight of his wife's face, that was always what helped to center him.

Rolling slightly to one side, Nate fished his cellphone from his pocket and called up his pictures. A notice in the screen's top right corner let him know his battery was down to thirty percent. Funny to think that without internet or cell reception, these devices were nothing more than expensive flashlights and photo albums. But there was a magic to looking at images of loved ones during good times. Focus hard enough and you could transport yourself back to that very moment, much like the picture he was looking at now—him and Amy standing on a sunny beach in Koh Samui, Thailand. They had gone there for their fifth anniversary, traveling from the mountains of Chiang Mai in the north to the tropical paradises down south. The next image was a selfie she had taken with his phone—the two of them having dinner on the beach, waves lapping mere feet from where they sat, giggling and enjoying pad thai and chicken green curry. He could smell it wafting up at them just as it had back then. Their smiles were a combination of love mixed with blissful ignorance of the future that awaited them.

And with that the cold swept back in. The number in the top right of his screen now read twenty-nine percent and he put his phone back to sleep. These images were his lifeline, the invisible cord linking him to his family, waiting for him in Rockford.

Nate glanced over at Dakota. She was awake now too and also looking at her phone, except she wasn't looking at pictures. She was reading something.

"What've you got there?"

She tilted her head, her eyes sleepy, her hair more disheveled than usual. "Just re-reading an old email."

Nate frowned. "How do you have reception?"

"Nah, I saved a copy of it in notes. Wanted to be able to read it whenever I could. It's the last message I got from Uncle Roger, about a week before the lights went out. He wasn't a softie by any stretch of the imagination, but it showed a side of him I'd never seen before. He'd even mentioned he was about to send me a special heartfelt message and not to worry, that his phone hadn't been hacked." She laughed at that.

"Emotions weren't Roger's strong point, I take it," Nate observed.

"I guess you could say that. It's true of most men, wouldn't you say?"

Nate's head bobbed up and down. "It's the way we were raised. And rightfully so. I can't remember the last time I cried and I'm not the least bit poorer for it." He reached out a hand, indicating her phone, grinning slyly. "You mind if I read what happens when uncles go soft?"

"Be my guest." She handed it over.

Nate went over it with great interest. "In case this here letter didn't make it obvious," Nate said when he was done, "the guy loved you like a daughter."

"Not more than his booze, he didn't."

Nate's face squished up with disapproval. "That's not very fair. Your uncle was an alcoholic, an addiction that's often more physical than it is mental. I'm guessing you've never seen what happens to a person who quits cold turkey? Their hands start to shake. They get hit with cold sweats. It ain't pretty. So you can stop beating him up over it. His struggle has nothing to do with you or how much he loved you."

Dakota became quiet for a moment. Then she said. "Yeah, I suppose you're right."

"I am," he said, winking. "We better get a move on before a fresh batch of Dylan's buddies shows up."

They exited the snow hut and both of them saw the dead hare at the same time.

"It's a snowshoe," Dakota observed. It lay next to the fire pit. A frozen smear of blood stained the white fur around its neck.

"A warning?" Nate wondered out loud. Although he knew the chances of anyone sneaking up on them in the middle of the night were slim.

"No, I think it's a gift," Dakota said. "From Shadow."

Grinning, he scooped the dead animal up off the ground. Its body was still soft, which meant the wolf had killed and left it there fairly recently. Removing her knife, Dakota began to skin the animal while Nate stepped away in search of a thick branch they could use to cook it with.

Along the way, Nate's mind traced over the events from last night. It seemed hard to fathom that a group of thugs would track them down in the midst of such chaos for revenge. There had to be something else going on. He thought back to Evan's work at the plant or any recent cases he'd taken on as a PI. Could any of those things have played a role?

After finding a branch that was just right, he returned to a fresh fire and a skinned hare. Dakota speared the animal and held it over the fire. The smell made Nate's mouth water. When it was done, both of them took turns eating. Nate let the girl go first. After all, she had done most of the work. Once she had eaten her fill, he did the same. Rabbit grease ran down his fingers and he licked it greedily. Without a doubt this was the best meal he'd ever eaten. What remained, they would keep for Shadow, a small reward for a much-needed gift.

When they were all done, Dakota fed Wayne some hay before they transferred whatever they could from Sundae's saddle bags. Seeing the dead horse, frozen nearly solid and covered by a few inches of snowfall, only served to reignite the anger Nate felt over the creature's senseless death.

With that done, Nate climbed onto Wayne's back and then helped Dakota do the same. The horse grunted under the extra weight. Nate rubbed the long, muscular side of the animal's neck. "Good job, buddy. You got this." *One part wishful thinking and nine parts prayer,* as his mother used to say.

Stepping out from the forest and onto the highway was like entering an Air Force wind tunnel. The blowing snow was coming directly at them, a sky swarming with tiny heat-seeking ice missiles. Nate bore the brunt of it, doing what he could to shield his face. Thankfully, Dakota had Nate to block most of the onslaught.

It wasn't long before they came to the clear outline of an SUV. It had skidded off the highway and been unable to recover or had simply become overwhelmed pushing against deep snow. Nate scanned the horizon in all directions. There was no sign of any living creature—of the two- or four-legged variety—in sight. He dismounted, his feet landing in a cloud of deep powder.

"Whatcha doing?" Dakota asked, now experiencing the full brunt of the wind and not liking it one bit.

"Wanna see something," he replied enigmatically. He used a gloved hand to clear the snow covering the driver's side window. The glass inside was opaque with frost. He tried the door handle and found that it worked. He stopped short, shuddering when he saw what was inside. A young woman in her early twenties was curled up in the passenger seat next to her newborn baby. Both of them were frozen solid. Icicles dripped from the tip of the woman's nose.

"What is it?" Dakota asked. Mercifully, her position on the horse meant she was too high to see what was inside.

"Nothing," he lied.

The keys were still in the ignition. He turned them. The dashboard lit up, but the engine wouldn't start. The mother had likely let it run until the tank had gone dry, waiting for a rescue that never came. Since leaving Byron, they must have passed over a hundred or more vehicles trapped along the way. How many more times had such a harrowing event played out along this stretch of road alone? He located two USB ports.

"Give me your phone and your charger," he said, his hand out.

"Huh?"

He bobbed his hand impatiently. The sight not three feet to his rear had affected him more than he cared to admit. It could just as easily have been Amy as a stranger. "Do you want your phone charged or not?"

She handed him what he asked for. Nate plugged in both phones and saw the lightning bolt indicate the devices were powering up. They wouldn't stay here more than a few minutes, but every little bit would count.

With Dakota sitting in the saddle, her head was a few feet higher than the SUV's roof. Nate noticed her eyeing something in the distance.

"You see someone?" he asked, the blood starting to pump a little faster.

She shook her head. No, not someone, something.

Nate opened the SUV door a little wider and used the nerf bar to prop himself up. His eyes swept over the terrain before them for a few moments before he saw it. The distinctive back end of a yellow school bus, tipped over on its side.

Chapter 32

Somehow the muscles in Nate's face, numb with cold, went completely slack. The phones had only been charging a few minutes when he ripped them out and stuffed them in his jacket pocket. He then jumped back in the saddle, digging his heels into Wayne's sides, shouting, "Rah. Rah!"

Wayne whinnied in protest, but ultimately obliged, moving forward as fast as the animal could carry them.

They were still fifty feet away and Nate was already searching for reasons this couldn't be one of the evacuation buses from the Byron Middle School. It was too small. Too clean. Too fill-in-the-blank. He needed something, anything to make it not be so.

Soon, through the blowing snow, he saw that the bus's emergency back door was hanging open. An accident of some kind had occurred, causing the bus to tip over. But the door meant at least some of the people inside had managed to get out. That was all he could make out from this distance. As they closed with the vehicle, he hopped out of the saddle with practiced ease, charging through powder near waist-high. He fought through it like a man in a heavy diving suit walking along the bottom of a lake. When he arrived, he clambered into the vehicle, looking for more proof it was a convoy from another school, maybe even another town. Given the vehicle's strange orientation to the ground, he found himself walking along the windows. Several of them looked to have shattered on impact, filling the compartment with small mounds of snow. Dakota climbed in behind him. She was smaller, nimbler and far better suited for this. She hurried past him and stopped about three quarters of the way to the front. She turned back, her eyes filled with surprise and maybe something else.

Is that sadness?

Nate hurried over and saw what she was glaring at so intently. A man in his seventies, maybe eighties, sprawled on his side. He must have died from the impact and been left behind. The scene must have been terrifying, chaotic. Two seats on, Nate found something else, something that looked familiar—a black duffel bag with the image of a man wielding two silver pistols. With shaking hands, he unzipped it, rifling through its contents until he came upon a black t-shirt stenciled with the words 'Battle Arena.' Nate held it in his gloved hand, a range of emotions welling up within him before he stuffed the shirt into his pocket.

"Belong to someone you know?" Dakota asked, her voice soft, almost reverent.

"To my nephew. My family, they were in this bus when it crashed. My pregnant wife too." One of his hands went instinctively to his stomach.

"I'm sure they're fine," Dakota said reassuringly. But even she couldn't completely hide the sliver of doubt she was feeling.

Quickly, they continued searching the rest of the bus. The only other casualty left behind was the driver. The guy was lying on the folding doors, still decked out in his District 226 jacket.

"Anyone you know?" Dakota asked, her gaze shifting between Nate and the driver.

Nate shook his head.

"That's good, isn't it?"

He wanted to tell her yes, wanted it more than anything he'd wanted in a long time.

"How many other buses were in the convoy?" she asked.

"Ten, maybe a dozen." His mind was too chaotic right now to think straight.

"I'm sure they made it," she said, overruling her natural pessimism.

Nate appreciated the effort. But he also wouldn't believe his family was safe until he saw them with his own eyes.

Chapter 33

Two hours later, they reached the outskirts of Rockford. The wind-battered sign along the side of the road told them so. For decades, this city of a hundred and fifty thousand had been one of the beneficiaries of the nuclear plant in Byron. And now it was also one of its victims. But passing that sign didn't mean they were out of harm's way. The exclusion zone included the bottom third of Rockford itself, which put the rendezvous point another five miles north of here. Cutting through a major city was not Nate's idea of a good time, either, especially one with Rockford's reputation. It had recently been ranked among the top twenty worst cities in America with a crime rate four times that of the national average. After the chief of police was arrested last year on charges of drug dealing and extortion, it became harder and harder to tell the good guys from the bad. To make matters worse, after the rot in the force had been uncovered, most of the good cops had moved out. Finding police in this city who weren't tied in some way to a criminal gang was harder than finding fur on a rattlesnake. Still, right now, none of that changed the necessity of what they were doing.

The path northward did offer some benefits. For starters, it would lead them right past the Javon Bea Hospital, the largest in the area. If Evan had been taken anywhere by ambulance, this would be the place. Along every mile of their journey so far, Nate had kept a careful eye out for the big boxy shape of an abandoned ambulance. Mercifully, he had not seen any.

Over the past few years, Nate's PI work had been conducted almost exclusively in Rockford. That meant he knew the city well, regardless of whether or not it was covered in a suffocating blanket of snow. It had also been a particularly profitable time for him with job offers pouring in by the bucketload. Not surprisingly, the vast majority had been for possible clients in Chicago—and why not with a city of nearly three million? But he had turned down each of those offers just as quickly as they'd come in. Life was too short to be humping up and down the mean streets of a major metropolis on a fast track to hell. Rockford was a tough nut, no doubt about it, but when your job was done you could still reasonably expect to return home in one piece.

There was another benefit to the years he'd spent working in Rockford. Connections. You got to know the cops, other private investigators and, above all, some of the more unsavory elements of the city's underworld. Folks who, as luck would have it, might be useful in helping them navigate the present situation.

It wasn't long before the snarl of wrecked and abandoned vehicles began to grow. And they weren't only seeing sedans and small hatchbacks either. Range Rovers, Escalades and a few Jeeps were also on display, only partly obscured by the never-ending flurries.

When they reached the intersection of Highway 20, the one that led to Interstate 90 and east to Chicago, it was abundantly clear most of the traffic had been heading in the other direction.

"I'm sure Uncle Roger had a lot to say about cities during a grid-down situation."

"Sure, he said to avoid them like the plague."

Nate laughed, stuttering when the sharp intake of cold air bit his lungs. "What Roger might not have considered are the nuclear power plants ringing this area. There are nine of them to the south and another four to the north. We know Byron and at least a few others have gone into full meltdown. Right now, the exclusion zone around the plant back home is only fifteen miles, but if that gets pushed anywhere close to fifty, and if that same fate follows the over two dozen plants in this part of the country, it doesn't leave folks with nearly as many places to go. Not to mention the forty-six other plants dotting the rest of America."

"So stay away from nuclear power plants," Dakota said, summing up. "That's the lesson."

"One of them," he acknowledged. "Especially given they were the very things targeted by the twisted, evil group that started this."

Slowly, laboriously, they crossed the Rock River and hung a left at a machine tooling shop. This was the industrial part of town and Kishwaukee was the main artery through southern Rockford. Following it north

216

would bring them to the city center and within striking distance of the hospital. Unlike in Byron, they soon encountered surprising signs of life—small groups of people, mostly in twos and threes, walking along the cluttered roadway, many of them carrying reusable grocery bags. They were dressed against the elements. Also, at least one member of every group carried a weapon, many of them sporting items. One guy had a bat, another what looked like a nine-iron golf club. Hockey sticks also seemed to be popular.

"These people don't seem all that worried," Dakota said. "Looks to me like they're heading to a communal sports event."

Nate made a mental note of the pistol in his waistband and how quickly he could draw it if need be. "Despite appearances, these people aren't out for fun," Nate told her. "They're searching for food. Least, most of them are. Others might be taking advantage of the chaos to loot. Though it's sometimes difficult to tell one group from another."

"The looters. Uncle Roger always said they would be the dangerous ones."

Nate agreed. "A starving man with a club won't hesitate to kill you for a can of tuna."

"Or a dead rabbit," she added, getting the point.

A few stragglers stopped and watched them pass. Two people riding into town on a horse was probably not a sight many of them had seen before.

The streets here were not nearly as tough to traverse as they had been back home. Population density, that was the difference. All of these folks stepping away from their homes to restock their shelves had helped cut a path along the sidewalks and roads. Nate suspected the further into town they drew, the easier the going would become.

"They don't know this area is within the exclusion zone, do they?" she asked, quietly.

Nate shook his head. "I suspect not. Most here are still in the dark, confused. All they know is this mess has been going on for the better part of five days now without any sign of letting up. If they stay here, it won't be long before strange things start happening to them. Things they don't understand. Bouts of dizziness and disorientation, diarrhea, nausea, vomiting. By the time their hair starts falling out, well…" His voice trailed off, swept away by a strong gust of arctic wind.

Two more hours passed. They were now approaching the center of town. Even so, this area was far more residential than what they'd encountered on the outskirts. The number of folks out and about had also gone up. There was even the occasional four-wheel-drive vehicle pushing through the deep accumulation. To the east came the rattle of distant gunfire. It wasn't the first time they'd heard that distinct sound since crossing into town. Quite the opposite. The closer they drew to the city center, the more frequent it had become.

Nate felt a surge of relief when he finally spotted the Javon Bea Hospital. The timing couldn't have been better. The painful throb in Nate's left knee was now coming in waves. Besides his own discomfort, Nate could almost hear Wayne's belly grumbling for a bit of hay. But there was something else. Their arrival in the center of town also represented another important milestone since it meant they were out of the current exclusion zone.

Another surprise greeted them as they approached the hospital—two, actually. The first was that some of the lights were still on. He knew the hospital had generators and a backup power system designed to deal with outages. The jury, however, was still out on how long that redundancy could last them.

The other thing they discovered was far less welcome, although not the least bit surprising given surprise number one. When you were the only show in town with electricity, you were bound to become inordinately popular. The line of cold and desperate people waiting to get inside stretched back around the corner. There was hardly a chance everyone here was really sick or waiting to see relatives. Most were simply trying to beat the cold any way they could.

A cordon of large men by the front door kept the masses at bay. Like bouncers they checked the crowd one at a time, peppering them with questions to weed out anyone who didn't have a good enough reason to be here. The vast majority were turned away, an act which on the surface seemed heartless and in direct opposition to a hospital's mandate until you considered that cramming lots of people together in one place only created a vector for disease. But the bar bouncer analogy only went so far, since the beefy guys blocking this entrance were also well armed.

Nate dismounted and approached a big guy wearing a North Face jacket and a black sailor's beanie.

"My brother's here," he said, moving forward only to be straight-armed in the chest.

"Line starts over there," the guy told him, gruffly, jabbing a finger from his gloved hand toward the starting point.

"Just check the list for me, would you?" Nate asked him. "His name is Evan Bauer. B-A-U..."

"You want some brain damage to go along with that hearing problem?" the guy threatened, his black pinprick eyes lost in his massive face.

"He was an engineer at the Byron nuclear plant," Nate persisted. He hadn't come all this way to be told no by some oaf. "He stayed after the core started melting down doing what he could to save your life and the life of everyone else in a fifty-mile radius. So the least you could do is check the damn list."

Those beady eyes wavered for a moment and then dropped to the clipboard in the man's hands.

"Bauer," Nate repeated, spelling it out.

"Yeah, fifth floor. Room 512," he said, waving him in. "But no weapons inside."

He was talking about the AR slung over Nate's shoulder. Nate went over to Dakota and handed it to her. A strong gust was kicking up again, making him feel terrible about leaving her out here. But if they couldn't bring weapons inside, they sure as hell couldn't bring horses.

"It's fine," Dakota told him. "Go see your brother."

"If you bring Wayne around the corner, you might be able to cut the wind a little."

She snorted laughter. "Thanks, Dad. Just go, but do it fast before I freeze to death."

Nate turned and hurried inside.

Chapter 34

He climbed the stairs to the fifth floor and found a hive of activity. Nurses in blue and purple scrubs hurried from room to room. In spite of the hazy glow from a midday sun, the hallway was dim. The hospital was probably on their final reserves of backup power and had cut as many superfluous electronics as they could. Notepad and pen replaced computer files. Clipboards replaced tablets. Nate let out a deep breath and watched a plume of cold air fill the space before him. It seemed even the heat was off.

Room 512 was easy enough to find. Nate was about to enter when a squat nurse popped out of nowhere, scowling up at him. "I'm sorry, sir, but you can't be here. This entire ward is for radiation patients only." He glanced down, noticing her bulky frame was made even bigger by the lead apron she was wearing.

Behind her, a figure that looked a lot like Evan lay in a bed protected by a see-through plastic tent. The sight left Nate with mixed feelings. On the one hand he felt an intense sense of relief and no small amount of joy at finally reconnecting with a loved one. But the deep sadness at seeing Evan in such a sorry state was almost just as strong.

"I'm here to see my brother," Nate said, pointing at the figure beneath the tent. "I was told he was in room 512."

The edges of the nurse's mouth curled downward for a moment. "Evan Bauer's your brother?"

"Yes. He was working at the…"

"We know, Mr., uh, Bauer—"

"Call me Nate."

"Your brother's in a medically induced coma. He was brought in two days ago suffering from broken bones and burns to ten percent of his body."

"Ten percent?" Nate repeated, horrified. For a reference point, he knew that the palm of a person's hand represented one and a half percent of their entire skin surface. "Will he live?"

The nurse's hardened glare softened a touch. "We're doing everything we can."

"I just need a minute with him," Nate said, a pleading quality to his voice. "It may be the last chance I get."

The nurse swiveled her head before heading to a nearby hook on the wall and bringing over another lead vest. "You've got five minutes. Put this on and take an iodine pill if you have one."

It wasn't the bubble of radiation outside she was worried about. He and Dakota had pushed past that particular threat. The danger here was new and unexpected. The victims from the Byron plant and the neighboring area lucky enough to be transported to hospital—they were the ones giving off the radiation here, his brother among them. Nate thanked the nurse, put the vest on and went to his brother's side. He could see well enough from here it was in fact Evan, buried under a thick wadding of blankets. The left side of his face was red and covered in blisters. Large chunks of the hair above his ear in the same area were missing, as though he'd visited a barber holding a serious grudge. He looked like crap, there was no other way to put it, and Nate wondered what he would tell Evan's wife Lauren when he saw her. Was it ever okay to lie in a situation like this? Tell her he hadn't been able to find Evan and let the man die in peace? What remained clear was that his brother was in no shape to travel. He was breathing on his own, that was good. But the poor guy was about a hair's breadth from folding his hand for good.

Nate watched the steady rise and fall of his brother's chest. "I'm not sure if you can hear me or not, bro. A part of me is surprised I made it this far myself. I went to the plant to look for you. A pair of trigger-happy guards shot up my truck and then told me you were already on your way here. In some ways you're the lucky one. It's frigid in here—no getting around that, I suppose—but out there things are so much worse."

The nurse popped her head back in and told him it was time.

He mouthed that he was almost done. "Amy, Lauren and the boys were taken to a shelter not too far from here. Well, I suppose far's a relative term. Not far used to mean driving there on a hot summer's day. The way things are now, one mile feels like ten, maybe more. The point I'm trying to make is that none of that distance stuff matters. We're gonna do what we can to stay close and check up on you as often as we can. Won't be long before we take you out of this place once and for all. In the meantime, just stay strong, brother." Nate reached under the plastic sheeting and squeezed Evan's hand.

"Mr. Bauer…"

Standing, Nate crossed to the door and stopped for one last look, just in case it happened to be his last.

•••

Minutes later, he was outside, buffeted mercilessly by an arctic wind. The line was still as long as it had been before, maybe longer. Present too were the muscle-bound bouncer types, screening who could and could not enter the hospital grounds. Dakota, on the other hand, was nowhere to be seen. Logically, she might have sought out a place nearby to escape the blowing snow. The hospital had a small inner courtyard, which Nate checked and found empty. He passed the front entrance again and followed the line around another corner and didn't find Dakota there either.

Where the hell did you go?

Amid his growing frustration, an array of possibilities occurred to him.

Was she around a different corner? Could she have sought out an empty house nearby? Or had she simply decided to set off on her own?

But here was the problem. None of those possibilities struck him as very likely. Here was a line of folks braving the cold for a chance to enter the hospital. So why would she flee from the elements or, worse, leave him behind?

Luckily, he still had his go-bag.

You might, but she has your AR, that little voice said.

"Nate?" a hooded figure from the line yelled out. "That you? Hey, man, the heck are you doing here?" The guy pushed back his hood, revealing a head of thinning hair and a set of pearly white veneers.

"Sanchez?" Nate replied, almost reflexively. Like Nate, Larry Sanchez was a former cop who had retired from the force in order to freelance. Mostly he did bodyguard work for rich kids and the occasional movie star. The man's name-dropping skills were legendary. He was also funny as hell once you got past his not-so-subtle need for self-aggrandizement.

Sanchez swung his head back, cackling with laughter. That was the other thing. The man had a sharp, distinctive laugh that always hung on the last note. Somewhere between a hyena and newborn baby. You hated the sound of it until you got to a point where you just couldn't wait to hear it again. "Would you believe this? The whole state's gone dark."

"The whole country, I'm afraid," Nate corrected him.

Sanchez recoiled and made the sign of the cross. He wasn't religious, but that never stopped him. "You're not kidding, are you?"

Nate shook his head, scanning the area at the same time.

"Please tell me you aren't on a job."

"You insane? I'm here to find my family."

"You sleep through the evacuation from Byron?"

Nate nodded. "Something like that. Most of my family, however, was taken to a temporary shelter on Winsor Road."

"The Victory Sports Complex?"

"That's the one."

"That may be, but Byron ain't the only town using us as a depot, amigo. Apparently, there's been such a huge influx, the city's running out of space to house everyone who's showing up. As it was, Rockford was struggling to keep its own citizens from dying even before the charity cases started flooding in. And the cold ain't the only thing bumping people off, if you know what I mean." Sanchez didn't need to wink, but he might as well have.

Nate understood perfectly well. Small as it was, Rockford had something of a reputation for criminal activity. With the normal structures of authority crumbling around them, it was a wonder the city wasn't in flames. Then Nate understood the reason. The cold. Stuff tended to rot a lot quicker the warmer things got. The same could also be said, for the rule of law.

"Listen, have you seen a young girl on a horse?"

"Sure have," Sanchez said without hesitation. "A chick on a horse ain't something you come across every day."

For some reason, the word 'chick' struck Nate like a pinprick between his lower ribs. But why? Was he already thinking of her as something of a daughter? He remained stoic. "You see which way she went?"

Sanchez motioned behind him. "I saw her come this way and head around the corner. She was talking to a couple guys by an SUV at some point. I assumed they were cops."

He must have noticed the flash of concern streak across Nate's features. Sanchez stepped out of line and both men headed in that direction. They were nearly there when they spotted the horse emerge from around the corner, walking slowly and without purpose. When they reached the horse, Nate saw one of the stirrups was up near the saddle. Dakota, however, was nowhere to be seen. The PI part of his brain was kicking into high gear.

It was starting to look as though someone had come along and abducted her.

But why?

They searched the area where she had likely been attacked, Nate's heart pounding wildly in his chest. He was just as terrified by what they might find as by what they might not.

The snow here was mostly undisturbed, save for a single spot where a mash-up of horses' hooves and human footprints gave the impression of a dance party. Kicking a light dusting of snow aside, Nate spotted a few droplets of blood.

"Last night we were camped out between Rockford and Byron when two men and a woman showed up. We thought they were friendly at first, but that was before I noticed the things they were saying weren't adding up."

"Cop's intuition, man," Sanchez bellowed. "It's a real thing. No one believes you when you tell them, but it is."

Nate went on to describe precisely how things had gone down the night before.

"A wolf?" Sanchez said, his gaze focused on a point somewhere over Nate's shoulder. "It look anything like that?"

Over near the street, Shadow stood, staring back at them. There was blood on the top of his head, like he'd been struck with a weapon of some sort.

"You two know each other?"

Nate frowned. "You could say that. Although I'm not entirely sure we're on speaking terms."

Sanchez didn't know what that meant, and Nate wasn't interested in filling him in on the backstory.

"Who'd you come here to see?" Nate asked, referring to the endless line.

"A cousin of mine tried to leave town and got stuck in his car overnight. Had to walk back on foot. Hands and feet were all frostbitten. The doofus didn't have the sense to bring mittens and proper boots in the off chance that his master plan flew off the rails. Anyway, I promised my aunt I'd check up on him."

"I could really use your help," Nate said, hating to call in the favor under these insane circumstances, but feeling like he had no other choice. "When I first found this girl, she was locked in a cage."

Sanchez's chin dropped, his mouth hinging open. "These guys wanted her awfully bad. Any idea why?"

"Can't say for sure," Nate replied, his mind recoiling from a host of sick and demented possibilities. While the ticking clock marking their escape from the exclusion zone had recently ended, he now realized another clock had suddenly taken its place. This one was much shorter and far more forbidding. Letting that particular timer run out guaranteed a terrible fate for his young traveling companion.

But Nate's motivation wasn't merely fueled by the simple fact that it was the right thing to do. Back on the trail he had inadvertently made Dakota a promise. If anything happened, he would come find her. And if there was one thing Nate tried never to break, it was his word.

Sanchez drew Nate's attention. "I think I know someone who might be able to help."

Chapter 35

Sanchez led them about five blocks from the hospital to meet one of his old contacts. It was rude to ride next to someone without a horse and so Nate had opted to lead Wayne on foot.

They were headed down a street with houses on each side when Sanchez glanced over his shoulder. "Your dog's still following us."

"Wolf," Nate amended. "And he isn't mine." Handing the reins to Sanchez, Nate pulled to a stop. He lowered himself onto one knee and held out a hand. Hesitantly, Shadow approached close enough for Nate to see someone had struck the animal's head with a club or a telescoping baton. It stood to reason that after trying to intervene, the wolf had been whacked in the skull for its efforts. But animals didn't normally show pain, not easily. The wolf's amber eyes stared back at him intently.

"Got any food on you?" Nate asked Sanchez.

Sanchez reached into his pocket and then put something in Nate's hand.

"A granola bar?"

Sanchez shrugged. "Hey, man, that's all I got."

Nate tore away the wrapper and held it out. Much to his surprise, the wolf came closer still, took the food from his hand, chewed it briefly and then let it fall to the ground uneaten.

Sanchez let out one of his famous cackles, spooking the wolf. Shadow backed off a few feet. "He's no vegan," Sanchez observed. "I'll give him that."

"You know, last night he wouldn't come near me without growling," Nate said, marveling at the sudden change.

"He wants something from you, man," Sanchez explained, matter-of-factly. "Can't you see that?"

"It's an animal. Most of the time, all they want is food."

Sanchez handed the reins back and ran his hand down Wayne's powerful neck. "I had the same problem with our miniature Schnauzer, Fonzie. Then one day Suzie brings home another named Chachi and wouldn't you know, Fonzie was suddenly my best friend."

Someone there is obviously a fan of Happy Days.

They continued walking while Nate pondered Sanchez's story. "So you're saying your dog was jealous?"

"I suppose that's one way to put it. Another was that he realized he suddenly had some competition. Up until then, the Fonz and Suzie outnumbered me. Don't ask me how, but the little guy realized the only way to avoid an all-out turf war was to get me on his side."

231

Nate grinned. "I think you put way too much thought into this."

"Spoken like a man who's never owned a dog."

"Amy's allergic," Nate shot back defensively.

"Laugh all you want, man," Sanchez derided him, throwing up his hands and spooking the horse, who flared his eyes and bobbed his head. "But I'm telling you. These things are smarter than we give them credit for."

"I don't know."

Sanchez halted and poked a finger into the puffy part of Nate's jacket. "That's what you don't get, man. You're part of his pack. Like it or not, you guys are family now."

Nate glanced back and noticed Shadow trailing a dozen paces behind, observing them with bright, almost human eyes. Difficult as it was to admit, maybe Sanchez was on to something.

They reached the house a few minutes later and Nate could see it was not what he had pictured in his head. The guy supposedly dealt weed and party drugs like ecstasy, nexus and poppers—precisely the sort of things kids ought to stay away from, but which seemed to draw them in anyway. Maybe because of this, a part of him had expected to find a dilapidated house in desperate need of a paint job. Out front would be a rotting deck, jammed with torn-up car seats or maybe a full-blown sofa. Instead, they had arrived at a three-story, old-school colonial with tall white columns. The place looked like something out of *Gone with the Wind* or maybe *Django Unchained*. Nate wouldn't be certain which movie applied best until they got inside. This guy seemed like more of a crime lord than a savior.

"You think this guy will be able to help us?" Nate asked, still not entirely sure why Sanchez thought this little pit stop was such a good idea.

"If anyone's got the pulse of this city it's Five-to-Ten." The door knocker was a rather delicate part of the male anatomy, two parts actually. Sanchez grabbed hold and slammed the door with it three times.

"Your old informant's got some interesting taste," Nate said. "But why's he call himself Five-to-Ten?"

"That's simple. It's the sentence range for drug possession with intent to distribute. But these days he goes by Five."

The door swung open to a burly black man wearing wide-rimmed sunglasses and a tanned suit. Nate watched as his gaze flit between the two men before passing behind them to Wayne. "What can we do for you gentlemen?"

"Big D, we're here to see Five," Sanchez said. "Official business."

"Tie your horse up outside," the bodyguard instructed him. "And wipe your shoes before entering."

Nate hesitated.

Seeming to read his mind, Big D flashed a set of impossibly white teeth. "Don't worry, friend. Ain't no one gonna steal that horse of yours. Not here."

Sanchez nodded and Nate did as he said, tying the horse to one of the white pillars. Not far away, Shadow stood in a depression of snow, staring back. "I'll try to bring you something," Nate told the wolf. In response, Shadow tilted his head and whined.

Once inside, a grand entrance was illuminated by dozens of candles. Dotting the foyer were pieces of antique furniture. Beyond that, a black and white marble floor led to a wide, circular staircase.

Big D led them up to the master bedroom. He opened both doors at once, like a page announcing a visitor for some European monarch.

Inside were more candles and lots of red velvet, more proof that getting rich selling dope didn't do a thing for one's sense of interior design.

A small, skinny guy sprang to his feet. He had long, stringy blond hair and a thick Brooklyn accent. He was also decked out in a double-knit sweater and baggy jeans. His heavy gold jewelry clanged whenever he moved. He waved for the bodyguard to close the doors and leave them.

"Sanchez, to what do I owe this pleasure?" the diminutive man said, a wry grin splitting his narrow features. The two shook hands. Turning to Nate, their host aimed a finger at him. "The hell's this? Guy looks like a Fed."

"He's not FBI or DEA," Sanchez assured him. "You aren't, are you?"

"Not the last time I checked," Nate admitted, still trying to get his bearings in this strange new world they had just entered.

Five scanned him up and down. "If you're vouching for him, Sanchez, that's good enough for me." Five stood there, nodding, then said. "Hey, where are my manners? Either of you guys want something to drink?" Five snapped his fingers and a scantily clad woman appeared out of nowhere. She crossed over to a nearby closet door and opened it to reveal a fully stocked bar.

"That's handy," Nate said.

Sanchez took a moment to pick his jaw up off the ground. "Your bartender's not half bad either."

Five snickered, his slight frame gyrating. "What'll it be then?"

"Oh, nothing for m—" Nate started to say before he felt a nudge from Sanchez. "Nothing light for me, is what I meant. Got any whiskey? Ten years or older would do nicely right about now."

Five nodded, impressed. He turned to Sanchez. "And you? Hot cocoa?"

Sanchez grimaced. "I'm off cocoa. How about a vodka tonic?"

"A mixed drink," Five said, arching one eyebrow. "How PC of you."

The half-naked woman brought them their drinks and then disappeared into the other room. They cheersed one another before settling into a plush semi-circular couch. "So, gentlemen, how can I help you today?"

Sanchez leaned over, scanning each of the doors to be sure the girl and Big D were gone. When he was certain he said: "Okay, let's cut the crap, shall we?"

Five straightened. "What are you—"

"Five's no drug lord," Sanchez interrupted, his voice low and filled with disdain. "He isn't really an informant either. He's more like—"

"A mole," Five said, completing the thought.

"A cop, if you want to be technical about it," Sanchez added. "But not as far as the bodyguard and the girl are concerned."

Nate shook his head and slapped the meat of his thigh, feeling like a man emerging from a wild dream. "You're undercover?"

Five sipped at his whiskey. "Deep. Make that real deep. Have been for years. When the lights went out, I could very well have called the whole thing off and headed home. And I might have if I had anyone there waiting for me."

The personal life of an undercover cop could often be summed up in two words. Divorced and alone.

Five went on, his thick Brooklyn accent already fading. "I suppose power of any kind is hard to walk away from, even when it isn't real."

Nate nodded, recalling the half-naked woman who had served them drinks. As foreign as Five's argument was, he could still see the allure of holding on through all of the present uncertainty.

"Besides," Five said, "over the last few days, Rockford's police force has pretty much vanished."

"Most of the young guys just went home, man," Sanchez explained, the distaste in his voice thick and unforgiving. "Said they were going to protect their families. But all they really did was leave the old-timers to bear the brunt. By day three, the nuke plants nearby were in full meltdown and the refugees from Byron and the surrounding towns started showing up in droves. Well, you can imagine how that went around here. Cops couldn't really use their cars to patrol on account of the snow. Sure, the SWAT team's got a single APC, but that beauty guzzles more booze than my mother-in-law."

"So why isn't there more chaos?" Nate asked, although part of him suspected he already knew the answer.

236

Five took this one. "If you think it's mainly because of this crazy weather, you're wrong."

"Those two brutes acting like doormen at the hospital," Sanchez said. "They weren't cops or even hired security. They're Jakes' guys."

"Jakes?" Nate said, recalling Dakota using the name, although he hadn't made the full connection. "You mean the former hitman?"

Sanchez and Five both nodded in unison.

Oh, crap, was all Nate had time to think. The guy was a verifiable psycho.

Jakes had worked for a big Chicago mobster and developed a reputation for cruelty and ruthlessness. Two years ago he'd been sent west to take back Rockford from the Russians and the Chinese. Systematically, he'd dismantled the rival gangs, not only through murder—of which there was plenty—but by infiltrating the local government. It was a trick Jakes had picked up from the Mexican cartels. Why bother fighting the government when you can become the government? Stuffing corrupt officials into City Hall and the police department, Jakes had all but assured his rivals would be picked off and sent to jail one by one.

How did Nate know all this? It was impossible to work the seedier parts of Rockford as a PI without coming face to face with Jakes' handiwork. If organized crime was Al-Qaeda, then Jakes was ISIS.

"Jakes ain't a hitman no more," Five told him, his eyes alight with fear or excitement, or maybe a bit of both. "He's moved up in the world. Graduated from low-level lieutenant to puppetmaster and now to local warlord. Since the lights have gone out, nothing happens in this city without his knowledge or approval."

Nate leaned back in his chair, the stark reality of their predicament slowly sinking in. A terrible tragedy for the country had become an opportunity for a man like Jakes. He was carving out his own minor fiefdom, deciding who lived and who died. A petty tyrant was the last thing Rockford or any city needed right now and yet, clearly, the rot had been going on for a while here, eating away at the foundations of the local government for so long that when the end finally came, it required no more pressure than a gentle push.

"You saying Jakes knows who took the girl?" Nate asked. "If so, what are the chances we can talk to him?"

"Whoa, amigo!" Sanchez said, waving his hands in the air like a man trying to clear away bad weed. "Weren't you listening? Jakes isn't gonna help us, man. He's the one who took that little girl."

Nate felt a crushing weight settle over his chest. "But what does he want with Dakota? She's nothing but an innocent child."

"It's not her they're after," Five answered. "It's the girl's uncle. Some dude named Roger. Word is, the guy's sitting on an arsenal of military-grade weaponry. Not only full autos. I'm talking fifty-cal machine guns and sniper rifles. Mortars and rocket-propelled grenades. The works. The guy was a freak and spent years building up enough to keep a man like Jakes in power for a long time."

"They wanna use her as a bargaining chip then?" Nate said, putting the pieces together.

"Something like that," Sanchez replied, stirring his vodka with the tip of his finger and then licking it. "They searched the guy's home in town and didn't find a thing.

Word is, he's got a cabin somewhere in the countryside. They think that's where he keeps the bang-bang stuff."

Nate rubbed his chin. "I see." Finding the girl in a cage and then getting attacked on the way to Rockford was suddenly taking on a whole new significance. "And if the girl doesn't lead Jakes to her uncle's stockpile, what then?"

Both men looked down. "It won't be good," Sanchez said. "If she's lucky, she won't suffer too much before they kill her."

That sinking feeling again, only this time it was blended with dread and served on ice. "I was worried you were gonna say that." Nate had a serious decision to make. On the one hand, he could go find his family and pretend like none of this had ever happened. Or he could add one more item to the list of bad choices he'd made in life.

Saving Dakota won't bring your sister back.

The words kept bouncing off the narrow confines of Nate's mind like that white digital ball from *Breakout*. Atari classics aside, he was beginning to realize there wasn't really a decision to be made. If he left Dakota to die a miserable death, he surely would not be far behind her. Guilt and shame had a way of gnawing at your soul. And as it was, Nate was clinging to the few ethereal scraps that remained of his own connection to a higher power. He remembered that look of surprise on the young girl's face when he'd told her she was worth rescuing. But deep down, he also knew the decision had already been made the second he found her missing.

Nate's eyes gleamed with anger and determination. "Where can I find Jakes?" he asked.

239

Both men looked at him as though he had lost his mind.

"You don't just go talk to Jakes," Five said, his voice resounding with no small amount of fear. "Not without an appointment, and even then…"

"Five is right, man. I mean, whatchu gonna do? Show up and demand he turn the girl over? You'll be dead before the sound of his laughter reaches your ears."

"I'm not gonna ask him," Nate told them. "I'm gonna go in there and take her."

"Man's got a deathwish," Five said, talking about Nate as though he wasn't even there.

"What's more, both of you are gonna help me."

"Ha!" Sanchez said, clapping his hands together. "Now you've really gone off the deep end, amigo."

"Just like me, both of you were cops at one time," Nate said. "Are you telling me you're ready to stand by while a young girl is murdered by a madman?" His burning glare, like two hot coals, passed from one man to the next. Neither of them could look him directly in the eye. "I see you've made your choice. I just hope you can both live with it." And with that Nate rose and walked out.

He got all the way to the front door before Sanchez caught up with him. "Listen, man, you know I would like to help you."

"This is my fight," Nate replied. "I get it. Maybe it's best if I do this alone."

"If there's anything else I can do to help…"

Nate's eyes rose to meet Sanchez's. "Actually, there might be."

240

Chapter 36

An hour later, they arrived at Sanchez's place, a quaint two-story home that featured a long driveway and a detached garage out back. Out front was a snow-covered porch with a swing and a set of summer chairs, also buried by the elements. The only thing missing were kids building snowmen in the yard. Speaking of which, they hadn't seen a soul on the streets since leaving Five's opulent, if tacky, colonial-style mansion.

They led the horse to the garage out back and set him up with a few fistfuls of hay and a half-dozen carrots. After they were done, the two men headed inside. Nate paused briefly to stomp the snow off his boots near the entrance, leaving them by the door.

"Where's Suzie?" he asked, regretting the question practically the second it had escaped his lips.

"Suzie's long gone, man," Sanchez said, hanging his jacket on a nearby hook. "She left me last year. Took the dogs and everything."

"No way! I'm sorry to hear that. I didn't know."

Sanchez ran his hands down the front of his face and let out a deep sigh. "How could you? It was right after we worked the Macomb job together."

Nate nodded. He remembered like it was yesterday. The wife of an upper-class businessman had thought her husband was having an affair. What she didn't know was that he had more than another woman on the side. The guy had an entirely separate family—two families, in fact, and he'd been splitting his time between each of them. A real multitasker, that was what Sanchez called him. But the job had chewed up months of their time putting all the sordid pieces together. Suzie must have grown tired of spending evenings and nights alone. It was something of an occupational hazard, one might say.

"Worst part about the whole thing," Nate told him, referring to the work they'd done for Mrs. Macomb, "was how she blamed us for what we'd found. Like we were making it up. She was the one who hired us, for God's sake."

Sanchez grinned, but there was pain behind his eyes. "Kill the messenger, right?" He stuffed his hands in his pocket and looked around. "Let me show you the stuff."

Nate followed his friend into the basement. It was nicely finished with a dark wood floor and a drop ceiling, but that didn't change how cold it was on their feet. Removing his phone, Nate shined the way with the flashlight app. They stopped before a work bench strewn with tools. Above it was a rack with three long rifles. The one in the middle caught his eye: H&K G36 with x3 optical sights and tac light on the front rail. It was a civilian version of the famous German assault rifle. Gas-operated, normally with a thirty-round mag (5.56×45mm NATO), Sanchez had outfitted this baby with a hundred-round drum magazine.

"You okay parting with the H&K?" Nate asked.

"She's my pride and joy," Sanchez admitted, "which is precisely why I think you should take her. I've always got the Colt AR and the SR-25." The latter was a semi-automatic sniper rifle that used the larger 7.62×51mm NATO round.

Nate removed the G36 from the wall mount, then stared through the scope at the light bleeding in through the basement's single window. The duplex crosshairs would do just fine.

"I got something else for you," Sanchez said, reaching beneath the work bench and coming out with a package wrapped in opaque plastic. "Might stop you from getting your head blown off in the first five minutes." He handed it to Nate, who tore it open. Inside was a set of MARPAT overwhites, essentially winter-themed camo he could put on over his existing clothes. A roll of white tape on the table could also be used on the rifle to keep it from sticking out.

Sanchez was staring at his old work buddy for what felt like a long time when he finally said, "She reminds you of your sister Marie, doesn't she?"

Nate set the camo gear down and said nothing. He knew his friend was talking about Dakota.

"She's about the age Marie was when she vanished. We've known each other for a long time, Nate. Wouldn't you say?"

"Sure. Ten years at least."

"That's right, and in all that time you never told me what happened. Given we might never see each other again, I'd say you at least owe me that."

The corner of Nate's mouth rose into a pained expression. He started to swallow and found what had always been a simple act had suddenly become far more difficult. "Marie was three years younger than me and a freshman in high school. I was in my first year of college. I guess you could say we got along as well as a brother and sister could be expected to, despite the gap in our ages. But we also didn't have a whole lot in common, save for our love of shooting. I'd bought a shotgun a few months earlier and had decided to introduce her to the joys of target shooting. Some people fire off a few rounds and find it's not their thing. Marie was different. She got a real thrill from feeling that wooden stock buried into her shoulder, from watching those watermelons disintegrate before our eyes as she pulled the trigger. It's a powerful experience for a young person. I'd gone through it myself a few years earlier and wanted her to also know that same sense of exhilaration.

"I was away at college back in those days, but whenever I'd come home she and I would head out to an empty field and blow away stupid stuff like shaken Coke cans and oversized watermelons. I kept the shotgun in my room back then, tucked under my bed, and told her never to touch it. One day, when I wasn't home, Marie broke those rules and took the gun out. She wanted to show her friend Bobby Hayes. Bobby was a year younger than she was and didn't have much in the way of friends. Looking back, I think Marie was trying to take him under her wing the way I had done for her. Wanted to give him

244

that same exhilarating experience she had felt that very first time. Ironically, she was in the middle of running Bobby through the safety procedures when the shotgun accidentally went off and blew away his right leg just above the knee. My sister panicked and ran for help, leaving poor Bobby in that clearing, screaming in agony. She didn't know much about tourniquets or how to deal with gunshot wounds. Hell, neither did I back then. Needless to say, the paramedics found Bobby not long after, lying right where he'd been shot. Said the kid had probably bled out in less than three minutes.

"She'd tried to do something good. Show the kid he was important and worth loving. But sometimes even the best of intentions come back to bite you where the sun don't shine. About a week after the kid was buried, Marie herself went out to the spot the kid died and never returned home. We spent the next few days searching high and low for any sign of her. Was she lost? Had she gone somewhere and taken her own life out of guilt? Or worse, had some sicko pulled up beside her on a desolate stretch of road and kidnapped her? We conducted more searches than you can imagine. Days stretched into months and then years. By then, we were no longer expecting her to come running through that door. And the reality we begrudgingly came to accept was that she was no longer alive. To this very day, I'd be just as happy to find my sister's body as I would to see her alive. It sounds like a strange thing to wish for, I know, but the human psyche craves closure. Living with that sort of mystery every single day has a funny way of gnawing at your soul, one bite at a time."

Sanchez's face was a mask of grief. "Oh, man, that's terrible. I couldn't imagine." He must have recognized something in Nate's face. "So when you dropped out of university after your injury, it was really you setting out to find her."

"Not consciously," Nate admitted. "But it was a big part of why, when I finally came home, I decided to become a cop."

Sanchez was quiet, thoughtful for a moment. Then: "You blame yourself, don't you? For her disappearance… for her death."

After she'd been missing for ten years, their family had pushed to have her legally declared dead. If time healed all wounds, then signing the paperwork to ratify your sister's demise had a nasty habit of tearing them open again.

"And why would I not shoulder at least some of the responsibility? I was the one who introduced her to it. Maybe if I'd had a gun safe, locked up tight, Bobby might never have gotten hurt and she might never have gone off—"

"You can't think like that. You'll drive yourself crazy. Coulda, woulda, shoulda, right? You told her not to and she broke the rules. I mean, you weren't even there."

"That's the problem, Sanchez. I wasn't there to protect her and I should have been."

Sanchez grabbed Nate by the shoulders. "So you think saving this girl will wash away your sins, is that it?"

"Something like that," Nate replied, his voice low and filled with resignation. "But before any salvation, I just need one more thing." His eyes rose to meet Sanchez's.

"Anything," his friend said.

"I need to know where to find Jakes."

Chapter 37

Armed with an answer to his question, Nate left Sanchez's place. He did so on foot, the sun having just set. Sanchez would keep an eye on his horse until he returned. There was no sense dragging the poor beast along only to leave him on the street to fend for himself.

Jakes was holding Dakota at the City Hall building on the corner of State and 2nd Street, which explained why Nate was positioned a hundred yards to the north, surveying the area through the scope of his rifle. The structure in his crosshairs wasn't so much one building, but two. The original section was eight stories tall, gleaming white and built in the 30s. The newer half had been added a decade ago in order to accommodate for Rockford's impressive growth.

But apart from leaving Wayne behind, Nate hadn't left empty-handed. Sanchez had hooked him up with one drum mag and six additional thirty-round magazines for the H&K. Along with that came a few extra mags of .45

ACP for the Sig and Colt Defender he carried. Finally, in case he managed to work his way through all that firepower, he'd brought his hatchet. Everything currently on him was housed in a white chest rig worn over his camo suit.

Before leaving, Nate had asked Sanchez if he'd be willing to head north to the sports complex shelter and check in on Amy and the others. He had also purposely told Sanchez to withhold news that Evan was in Rockford at the Javon Bea Hospital. That would have to wait, since he didn't want to risk Lauren heading out into a squall in search of her husband. Besides, with the real authorities sidelined, the human animals bottled up in a city without power were bound to erupt at any moment.

Speaking of beasts, Nate had hardly settled into his recon nest when he caught the sound of someone or something sidling up from the adjacent alley.

Shadow whined and licked his hand. Nate reached into his pocket and pulled out a small handful of kibble he'd grabbed from Sanchez's place.

"I had a sneaking suspicion you might show," Nate said, grinning as he held out his hand. "Here, compliments of Fonzie and Chachi."

Shadow sniffed at the niblets before digging in.

"There you go." He watched the wolf finish, running his powerful tongue down Nate's fingers and along his palm. "You better lie low, buddy. You won't wanna be anywhere near what's about to go down, trust me."

The wolf stared at him, licking his lips.

Nate returned to his reconnaissance. Out front, two large men stood guard. Although standing wasn't entirely accurate, since they were shifting from side to side, stomping their feet in a vain effort to root out the cold. That was good for Nate. Their discomfort was a distraction he could use to his advantage.

Every so often, he witnessed an array of figures entering or exiting the building. Some appeared to be security, while others were simply regular folks, perhaps petitioning Jakes to help with food or to admit a loved one to the hospital. But why they had come and where they were going, Nate could not say for certain.

With nearly all traditional forms of communication down, it was hardly any wonder Jakes was a busy man. After wresting control of Rockford from the rightful authorities, maintaining a firm grip on law and order— however draconian that might be—required a near-continuous stream of information. That explained the flow of people in and around City Hall. And yet, in the time Nate had been observing the building, he hadn't seen anyone matching Dakota's description coming or going.

Rising from his perch, Nate pushed through the alley and north on 3rd Street. He then cut around behind City Hall, searching for a back way in. Poking out of an alley, he could see this part of the street was deserted. That was good, but what he lacked was perhaps the most vital part of any rescue mission: intel on what to expect inside. Sanchez and Five seemed confident Dakota was in there somewhere. But on what floor and, more importantly, in what room? The first rule of any successful snatch-and-grab mission was getting in and out without ever being seen. A firefight was a telltale sign things were no longer going to plan.

On a whim, Nate pulled the Geiger from his jacket pocket and switched it on. They were out of the exclusion zone, he knew that, but that didn't mean they were free of any and all radiation. To his surprise, the needle spiked and the machine registered an intense amount of crackling static. But how could this be? He had expected to find it a touch above background, not several times that. Could the Byron plant's situation have worsened in the time since his escape? And if so, had the exclusion zone perimeter been pushed even further?

Unforeseen as it was, the discovery only reinforced the dire need for speed. And not only to free Dakota. There was no doubt, once a guy like Jakes squeezed the information out of her, the girl's predicament would go from very bad to hellish in a heartbeat. Being stuffed back in a cage would be Christmas compared to what a psycho like Jakes surely had in store.

A voice came from behind him. "Is that a Geiger counter in your pocket or are you just happy to see me?" There was just enough ambient light to see it was Sanchez.

"The hell are you doing here?" Nate asked, shocked and yet at the same time happy to see his friend. "And how long have you been itching to spring that line on me?" His surprise grew when he noticed Sanchez was wearing a chest rig and carrying an AR-15.

"I thought about what you said and you're right," Sanchez told him. "As much as I tried, I couldn't just sit back and do nothing. I may not know this girl, but next time it might be someone I care about."

"Did you get a hold of Amy?" Nate asked, already dreading the answer.

Sanchez shook his head. "I had a choice, either save you from killing yourself or check on your wife. I chose option one. You're welcome."

"You're thanked," Nate said. "Listen, you remember a few years back when I asked you to help me with the Johnson case?"

Sanchez perked up. "The jealous boyfriend who was holding the client hostage, threatening to kill her unless we tore up the evidence of his infidelity and told her we'd made the whole thing up? That Johnson case?"

"That's the one. The more I think about it, the more I realize it's also the way we need to play this."

"No negotiation. Go in strong and shoot to kill."

Nate grit his teeth and nodded.

"All right, amigo," Sanchez said. He plucked a necklace of St. Christopher from under his shirt and kissed it before pulling the action on his rifle. "Lead the way."

Nate looked at him. "Where's my good luck charm?"

Sanchez winked. "You're looking at him."

They exited the alley, sticking close to the buildings as they struggled through the heavy snow. Reaching the intersection, Nate scanned in both directions. They could see one of the two guards, standing out front, showing them his back. But the guy's incessant movement to keep himself warm meant that every few seconds he would turn around. Calculating the distance along with their speed, he figured there would be a sixty-second period crossing the street where they would be exposed. Nate observed the man's patterns. Two stomps of the feet followed by a glove rub, a lungful of warm air blown into cupped hands and a quick glance over his shoulder. Every time was nearly the same routine. Nate felt the pulse in his neck quicken.

The guard's quick glance came. Then, as soon as the guy's back was turned, Nate gave Sanchez the signal to move out. Both men hurried across the street as fast as they could. Ammo weighed more than most people realized, especially when you were lugging it over difficult terrain. Nate never imagined the streets of Rockford would ever be described in that way. And yet the last week had been nothing but one surprise after another.

The two men were nearly halfway across when the guard began to turn. Nate gave the order to drop and at once they dove into a bed of deep powder. A few seconds later, he lifted his head enough to peek out. The guard was still looking their way, his forehead scrunched up.

He's seen us. Has to have. Better to rise up now and start firing rather than be shot lying down. The best chance of winning any shootout was being first to get your rounds downrange.

Then another, stronger voice told him to chill out. There would be plenty of time to blow cover inside once the bullets started flying.

The guard turned away and Nate hesitated a second or two on the off chance it was a ruse. When he saw that it wasn't, he reached back and tapped Sanchez. They rose, pushing hard to close the distance between them and the back of the building.

At their destination, a low metal staircase led to a glass door. Nate and Sanchez made it and hugged the wall. Careful to keep out of sight, they climbed the few steps, one at a time, their heavy boots crushing snow into the metal grate beneath their feet. Nearing the top, Nate reached for the handle at the same moment that

252

the door swung open on its own. Retracting his hand, he remained still. So too did Sanchez behind him.

A beefy guy in a black parka sprang out. Anticipating the cold, he was already wearing the hood of his parka up. Otherwise, they would have been spotted for sure. The guard stood less than four feet away, giving them his back. He was stabbing both hands in his pockets, swearing under his breath. A moment later, he found what he was looking for. A pack of cigarettes and a lighter. He shook one out, stuck it between his lips and lit the end.

"Damn sonofabitch don't own me," the man murmured, spitting over the railing and watching it swallowed in a mound of powder below. "The hell does he get off?"

The G36 was strapped diagonally across Nate's back. Not that it mattered, there was no practical way to swing it into action in such close quarters. The Glock 21 would have to do. He pulled the weapon with one hand and lunged forward in a burst of speed, grabbing the back of the smoking guy's parka hood with the other. A startled sound was the only thing that escaped the man's lips before Nate yanked him off his feet. The guy was big, which explained the crack as his lower back struck the edge of the top stair. He opened his mouth to holler in pain. Nate was ready, muzzling him with the palm of his gloved hand. Up came the Glock, the barrel pressed against the center of the big guy's forehead. His eyes were watering just as much from the pain in his spine as it was from the intense fear coursing through every twitching fiber of his being.

"I'm gonna remove my hand in a second and you're not gonna scream, are you?"

253

His eyes, already wide, darted from left to right as he shook his head vigorously.

"Good. Now, how many of Jakes' men are inside?" Nate eased his hand off the guy's mouth.

"I can't breathe."

"That's not what I asked you."

"A lot," he replied, panting. "More than usual."

"And the girl, where is she?"

"Girl? We got lots of girls."

"White. Fifteen years old. Five foot three or so. Suffers from a bit of an attitude problem. Ring any bells?"

A light went on. "Oh, her. Yeah, I heard Jakes killed that one. She was mouthing off and…" The thug's voice trailed off, understanding in that moment he might have said too much.

"Killed?" Nate repeated, his voice icy cool, his heart suddenly devoid of mercy. He shoved the barrel deeper into the man's flesh and pulled the trigger. The Glock made a muffled, but audible sound.

"Oh, man, someone heard that for sure," Sanchez scolded him. "We gotta move before this place is swarming."

Nate sprang to his feet, holstered the Glock and swung the G36 assault rifle around. Sanchez pushed past him and pulled open the door. In Nate went, his anger no longer seething. It had already morphed into a mushroom cloud of white-hot wrath. In a matter of seconds, the mission had transitioned from find and rescue to search and destroy.

Chapter 38

Now inside, Sanchez grabbed him by the arm. "Hey, man, if it's true the girl's dead, going in there won't bring her back. I say we get out of here while we still can." He paused. "Think of your family."

"What good will I be to them if I tuck tail like a coward and run? You wanna go, I won't hold it against you. This is my fight."

"I shoulda known when I saw that crazed look in your eye there'd be no reasoning with you."

Nate leveled his weapon down the corridor, switched on the tac light at the end of his rifle and pressed on. They hurried down the narrow hallway, passing through a set of doors and into an expansive lobby. Had Nate not been so consumed with revenge, he might have stopped to gawk. It was an art deco lover's wet dream—black limestone floors opposite a high glass ceiling with Ohio sandstone walls. At either end were giant murals depicting the city founders dressed in nineteenth-century garb and wielding pickaxes.

Suddenly, the frantic sound of shouting along with the clatter of heavy boot treads echoed back at them. Nate and Sanchez were out in the open. The area was bare except for a series of leather couches and seats to their right.

A half-second later, three men in thick coats staggered into the lobby. For a moment, it appeared they might be heading toward the front entrance. Then one of them skidded to a stop and shouted at his companions. "They're over he—"

His full warning was interrupted by two quick rounds from Nate's rifle, the sound of gunfire nearly ear-popping. The rounds rippled the fabric of the man's jacket, cutting power to his legs. He dropped. Sanchez bagged the one behind him as Nate cut right, firing from the hip as he headed for the couches. His weapon kicked like a mule in heat.

Seeing his two buddies torn to shreds, the third and farthest gunman should have done the smart thing and run away, but he didn't. Instead, he went for Nate, riddling the soft leather couch with bullets. In response, Nate dropped and hugged the ground. Staring out from beneath the sofa, he had a clear view from the man's feet to his knees. The moment he swiveled his rifle in position, that was where he aimed, his rounds firing out from beneath the couch. One shot struck the guy's kneecap while another from Sanchez slammed into his chest, collapsing his lung. He fell over, gasping for air.

When the shooting was done, Nate got up and approached the dead and dying. Only the last guy was still breathing.

"Where's Jakes?" Nate asked.

Blood ran from the corner of the man's mouth. He began to speak but it was little more than a whisper. Nate drew closer.

"Top floor. He's waiting for you," the man said, between deep, labored breaths.

A mercy shot from Sanchez finished him. "What'd he say?"

"Jakes is waiting for us."

The corners of Sanchez's mouth turned down. "The hell do you suppose that means?"

"I'm not sure," Nate said, swallowing down his growing concern. He then quickly searched the bodies and noticed they were using AR-15s. He threw Sanchez a few extra magazines before they carried on.

No power meant no elevators. It also meant at least eight flights of stairs.

They entered the stairwell. "I hope you kept up that gym membership."

A guilty, worried look spread over Sanchez's face. Together, they glanced up the center of the u-shaped stairwell.

Sweat was already pouring down Sanchez's face. "Oh, man."

Both of them peeled off their white camo and heavy jackets. From here on, mobility and maintaining stamina would be key.

They began to ascend and had barely made it past the first floor when they heard a metal door slam somewhere above them. That was quickly followed by boots clomping down two risers at a time.

Nate and Sanchez crept up slowly, keeping their angles clean. The element of surprise could very well be the difference between life and death. Nate's pulse ratcheted up as they drew closer.

A noise from behind startled them. Someone was coming out onto the second-floor landing. Nate swung around and saw one of Jakes' thugs brandishing a shotgun and a bright shock of bleach-blond hair. For a moment, Blondie looked just as startled as they did. He recovered quickly and up came his shotgun right as Nate pulled the trigger God only knew how many times. Blondie took one to the gut and two to the chest. He staggered back, peppering the riser just below them with double-aught buck.

No two ways about it, this was a terrible position to be in. Threats coming from multiple directions meant they were unable to focus their fire. It also increased the chances one or more of Jakes' men could pop out above or below them at any time.

Now the shouting from above got louder. Unfortunately, the element of surprise had gone out the window the second Blondie made his grand entrance. Nate switched to a fresh magazine and made sure to keep a tight angle. They also made sure to hug the outer wall so no one could shoot them from above.

Then shots rang out, ricocheting around the stairwell. It seemed these guys weren't as dumb as they looked. They knew well enough charging into another man's firing line was a damn good way to make yourself dead. Nate also realized moving forward would be a hard slog, a kind of chess game where each side sought to outmaneuver the other. The smart play was to press on, slowly, methodically.

If they were the two-bit drug dealers and hoodlums he thought they were, that was precisely what they would be expecting. And that was precisely why Nate broke into a run, scaling two risers at a time, keeping his weapon always trained on the next stairway and landing beyond. Shadows thrown from their tac lights helped to confuse and disorient the enemy.

Behind him, Sanchez struggled to keep up, huffing and puffing like a man on the verge of cardiac arrest.

The charge seemed to have the desired effect. The first two thugs were in the midst of running away when Nate gunned them down. Two others slammed into each other after deciding to tear off in opposite directions. Sanchez got a piece of them. Another couple escaped onto the seventh floor, the door slamming shut behind them. But giving chase wasn't in the cards, not yet. This was not the time for rabbit holes. Nate's primary objective remained the same: place a tight grouping of bullets between Jakes' eyes. Only when that was done—God willing—would he allow himself the gratuitous luxury of finishing off the rest of the man's crew.

At last, Nate and Sanchez reached the eighth floor. What they found there was a veritable maze of offices and cubicles. Webs of shadow vanished and reappeared before the sweep of their tac lights.

In the distance, the warm glow of candles hinted at a presence up ahead. Nate and Sanchez moved forward, cautious, but ready.

They reached a large office filled with expensive oak furniture. In one corner behind a bookcase was the faintest hint of a door. It appeared to lead to another office, or perhaps to a bathroom. They were about to pull out when two figures emerged, their hands raised in the air. Nate leveled his weapon and saw Five. Next to him was Dakota, a piece of duct tape over her mouth. She was murmuring from beneath the tape, her eyes wide with terror. Or was that something else? The whole scene was downright confusing. He'd thought she was dead. But here she was, next to Five, and both of them prisoners, their arms up.

"Anyone turns around and you all die," the gravelly voice said from behind them. Nate had only heard Jakes speak once, to a reporter after beating a murder rap in Chicago. But it was the kind of voice that sent bony fingers dancing up the back of your neck and that was precisely the feeling he had right now.

"Now, put your guns down," Jakes ordered them.

Dakota shook her head vigorously. He didn't need an interpreter to know she was telling him not to do it. The real question was whether or not he'd be able to draw his Glock and spin around before taking a bullet in the back. His right hand began inching toward his pistol grip.

"Why should we? You're just going to kill us anyway," Nate said, hoping to buy time. "Let Dakota and Five go and we'll do it."

A low laugh filled with menace. "You don't really get it, do you? Five is the reason I knew you were coming."

Nate glowered at the small man before him. "You rat!" he shouted.

"Nothing worse than a crooked cop, man," Sanchez said with disgust.

Five cackled with laughter before pulling out a pistol from his waistband and aiming it at Dakota's head. He tsked, wagging his index finger at them. "They still haven't pieced it together, have they? Jakes doesn't run Rockford. I do. He works for me. The chief and I were running things until he got put away. That left yours truly."

Sanchez's eyes widened in shock.

Five and Jakes both snickered. "Surprised, aren't you? Now set your weapons on the floor, all of them."

Nate and Sanchez did so. Soon two pistols and two assault rifles lay before them.

"Your backup gun too," Five said, annoyed.

Nate grit his teeth and complied.

Five waved the barrel of the pistol wildly and then settled it against Dakota's temple. She closed her eyes, and Nate couldn't tell if she was praying or wishing for all of this to be over. "Your little friend here's been trying to tell us she doesn't know where her uncle keeps his cache of high-powered weapons. And until you came knocking, we were almost starting to believe her." Five turned his attention to Nate. "I'm a reasonable man. A very generous man. You don't believe me, ask Jakes."

"It's true," Jakes said.

Five eyed Nate up and down. "A real go-getter. I respect that. I could use someone like you in my organization. Probably won't come as much of a surprise, but ever since the power's been off, business has been booming. So here's the offer and I suggest you consider it carefully because I won't be repeating myself. You help me get my hands on that cache of weapons dear uncle Roger's been hoarding. In exchange, I'll see to it you and your family live in Rockford like royalty." Five pressed the barrel deeper into Dakota's flesh. "And as a bonus, I won't blow this pretty little girl's brains all over that wall."

Dakota began to mumble.

Five rolled his eyes and mocked Dakota's attempt to speak from under the strip of tape covering her mouth. "She's got a real mouth on her," Five said, still basking in the glow of his own dumb joke. "You leave it up to me and I'd just as soon finish her off nice and slow."

Dakota continued mumbling. Five reached over and tore back part of the duct tape covering her mouth. "What the hell is it? Can't you see the men are conducting business? You just wanna chime in with your two cents, don't you?"

"Yeah, and here they are," Dakota snapped. "Screw you and your stupid offer." In a blur of motion, she slammed both of her arms down on the hand Five was using to hold his pistol.

From behind Nate came a grunt of surprise from Jakes. Time slowed to a deadly crawl. Any second now, Dakota was going to be shot dead, along with Nate and Sanchez soon after. With the hatchet gripped tightly in his hand, Nate spun on his heels and swung it down, burying the carbon fibre blade into the top of Jakes' skull. At once, the man's eyes rolled up to whites and he let out a groan before crumpling to the ground. By the time Nate turned around, two stray shots rang out from Five's gun as he and Dakota struggled over it. Then came a third shot. This time it was from Sanchez. Five let go and brought both hands up to his throat, blood rushing out from between his fingers.

Nate reached Five right as the crooked ex-cop hit the floor, writhing.

262

Sanchez came to join them and stumbled. Nate caught his friend, regarding him with a puzzled. Then they both glanced down at the same time to see the bloodstain blooming on Sanchez's shirt.

"Oh, crap, man," Sanchez said, sputtering blood. "The little prick got me."

He tensed in pain and set himself down. Already the flesh on Sanchez's face was growing pale, his lips a light shade of blue. Five's bullet must have hit an artery.

"Just give me a minute," Sanchez requested, as though a short break was all he needed.

"We gotta get you help," Nate said, preparing to lift his friend up on one shoulder, his bum knee be damned.

Sanchez waved his hand dismissively. "Don't be a fool, man. I won't make it to the ground floor, let alone through all that snow."

Nate could see the life draining out of him at a frightening pace. Sanchez gripped his hand. His fingers were already cold. An insane amount of blood was pooling on the floor beneath him.

His friend's voice was down to a whisper. "I'm glad."

Nate squeezed back. "About what?"

"That I stayed." Sanchez smiled, squeezing something into Nate's hand. It was the pendant of St. Christopher he always kept around his neck. "Hopefully this'll do you more good than it did me. Now go get your family. And find somewhere they'll be safe." Sanchez barely got the words out before his grip loosened and then fell away.

By contrast, Five continued to sputter away on the floor nearby. Dakota remedied that particular inequity with two shots to the head from Five's own pistol. This time, when the chips were down, she hadn't been paralyzed with fear, Nate realized. At least some good had come out of all this death. He pulled her into a hug, sad for the friend he had lost and relieved for the daughter he had found.

Chapter 39

With Jakes and Five dead, the two of them headed back to the lobby. The glass doors at the front entrance, shattered in the firefight earlier, were now letting in cold air and blowing snow. Their feet crunched on broken shards when they heard a weapon being cocked.

Both of them turned at once to see two fresh bodies on the ground, which was strange because Nate remembered only encountering three thugs in the lobby. Also observing the fresh carnage was a young man, somewhere in his late teens, early twenties, holding a pistol. He was one of Five's men, clearly still ignorant that his boss lay dead up on the eighth floor. The kid fought to steady his quivering hands. Then from out of the darkness came a low, threatening growl. All three of them looked at once to see a pair of glowing eyes staring out at them from a deep pocket of darkness. Except that feral stare wasn't locked on them at all. It was aimed at the young man with the gun.

"I suggest you do as he says," Nate told the kid, who looked like he might have just wet himself. "Whatever you do, just don't—"

Before Nate could finish, the kid stuffed the gun in his pocket and tore off for the closest exit. Shadow gave chase.

"I was about to say 'run,'" Nate said, finishing the sentence.

The corner of Dakota's mouth turned down. "You did try to warn him."

They pushed out into the cold, the sound of distant screams swallowed by the howling wind. They didn't need to wait for Shadow. The wolf was his own boss. He would find them when he was good and ready.

Chapter 40

Their next stop was the Victory Sports Complex, a glorified indoor soccer field half a mile away. It was here that the refugees from Byron had been sent. His family was among them and now that Dakota was safe, Nate's only desire was to see them again.

As he trudged laboriously through the snow-filled streets, Nate's mind kept returning to the overturned bus they'd found on the highway leading into town. The sight of Hunter's backpack in the wreckage hadn't simply shaken his confidence his loved ones were safe, it had knocked it down and kicked shards of ice in its face.

Nate and Dakota walked for close to an hour before the peak-roofed aluminum structure finally came into view. And all at once Nate's heart sank.

"What's wrong?" Dakota asked, noticing the change.

"The buses are gone," he said, his voice tight with emotion.

267

"Don't worry about it. They're probably around back."

The girl had offered him a thin reed of hope and he decided to take it. He could see the vague shape of cars buried under mounds of snow in the parking lot. That had to mean something.

Approaching a set of glass doors, Nate spotted the flame from a single candle inside. It was late evening, which meant whoever was here might very well be asleep.

Nate switched on the light from his cell phone and pushed his way into the sports complex.

Unlocked doors and no visible security. None of this was setting his mind at ease. For a moment, they stood at the entrance, taking in the darkened space before them. Murkiness aside, it was the silence that disturbed him most. Where was the coughing, the snoring, the sound of cots creaking as folks shifted position?

The beam of light from his phone was quickly swallowed up by the enormous space. And yet the few feet of visibility it had afforded made one thing perfectly clear. The sports center was virtually empty.

Nate's attention shifted to the solitary source of light in the distance. He and Dakota headed toward it, feeling like moths drawn to a flame. Not a moment later, he bumped his leg on an empty cot and cursed. Scanning around, he could see now vacant cots were everywhere, along with discarded blankets and possessions left behind.

Ten meters away, a lone figure came into focus, lying still in the candle's warm glow. Fighting back waves of sadness and disappointment, Nate weaved through the sea of empty cots.

They arrived at an old man, his skin dotted with sunspots and wrinkled with age. He opened his eyes.

"Have you come to kill me?" His voice, barely a whisper, betrayed no sign of fear. Either way, he seemed like a man resigned to his fate.

"No," Nate replied evenly. "I'm sorry to disappoint you. I'm looking for my family."

"There were a lot of families here," the old man said, unable or unwilling to sit up. "But not anymore."

"What happened?" he asked.

"The radiation," he replied. "We were told it wasn't safe anymore. That we had to keep moving."

"Do you know where they were sent?"

The man's head made a slow nod. "Natural History Museum."

"Huh? Where's that?" Dakota asked.

Nate's voice became low, somber. "Downtown Chicago."

"Oh, no," she said, before she could catch herself.

But Nate couldn't really blame her since he had just been thinking the same thing. Any major metropolis was a dangerous place in a grid-down situation. It was hardly a secret that some cities were worse than others. He knew Chicago well, a city as renowned for its beauty as it was for its crime. He had walked its inner-city streets as a beat cop for longer than anyone should be expected to. With this in mind, Nate began to steel himself for what lay ahead. Saving his family now meant entering a veritable hornets' nest.

Dakota turned her attention back to the old man. "Why didn't you go with them?"

"I'm not made for a life on the run," he explained, trying his best to smile and managing to hold it for nearly a full second. "I should never have left Byron. At least then I could have died in my own bed."

"Is there anything we can do?" Nate asked.

A twinkle of gratitude formed in the old man's eyes. "I fully expected to die alone in the dark. Maybe you could sit for a minute, hold my hand."

"Sure thing," Dakota said, settling down on the edge of the man's cot and folding her delicate hand into his.

Chapter 41

After the old man passed, they returned to Sanchez's place, still processing everything that had just happened. The loss of Sanchez was hard enough, but to have Nate's family slip through his hands made it all the more difficult to bear.

The next morning, after stocking up with weapons, ammo and food, Nate found an old framed picture of his friend on the wall, a little five-by-seven job. He removed the photograph and stuffed it into his pocket.

"What's that for?" Dakota asked.

"I'll do something on the road to honor him," Nate replied. "Or maybe I'll just keep it on me. A remembrance of a friend who made the ultimate sacrifice." The necklace of St. Christopher was also around his neck and there it would remain.

"You're going to Chicago now, aren't you?" she asked. "To find your family."

Given the state of the country, it was the last place on earth any sane person should be heading. If Rockford was coming apart at the seams, he couldn't imagine how things would be in a city of nearly three million. But sometimes you had to crawl through hell to get to heaven. And rather than say a word, he simply nodded. There was no other choice. "And you?"

"If my uncle's still alive, I have a good idea where he might be."

Nate nodded and zipped up his jacket. "Good. If it's along the way, I'll take you there."

"It is," Dakota said, smiling, her delicate features wavering in the soft winter light spilling in from outside. "I can't think of anyone else I'd rather have with me."

Nate favored her with a brief glance and a wink. He shouldered his rifle and said, "So what do you say we get going?"

Thank you for reading America Offline: Zero Day!

Be sure to check out the rest of the series now available for pre-order!

America Offline: System Failure (Mar-2020)
America Offline: Citadel (May-2020)

Other books by William H. Weber

The Defiance Series
Defiance: The Defending Home Series
Defiance: A House Divided
Defiance: Judgment Day

The Last Stand Series
Last Stand: Surviving America's Collapse
Last Stand: Patriots
Last Stand: Warlords
Last Stand: Turning the Tide

The Long Road Series
Long Road to Survival (Book 1)
Long Road to Survival (Book 2)

Made in the USA
Columbia, SC
08 December 2021

50754104R00171